THE
BOOK
OF
ELLISON

THE
BOOK
OF
ELLISON

EDITED BY

ANDREW
PORTER

ap algol press

Published by
ALGOL Press
P.O. Box 4175
New York NY 10017

First Edition, October 1978, consisting of 1800 paperback copies and
a limited edition of 200 hardcover copies.

Quality paperback ISBN 0-916186-08-3. $5.95
Hardcover ISBN 0-916186-07-5. $15.00

For my mother

INTRODUCTION
Isaac Asimov

Judging the value of a man's writing is a highly subjective task and comparisons come out different. Some people, for instance, might think that Isaac Asimov's stories are better than Harlan Ellison's. I think so, for instance, and who should know better? I must admit, on the other hand, that other people think Harlan's stories are better than mine—and as soon as I find those two guys, I'm going to kill them.

Charisma, however, is something else again. That is an absolute. Whether you love Harlan or hate him (and there is no in between) and whether he loves you or hates you (and there is no in between there, either) you've got to admit he's got it.

He is never anywhere without your knowing he is there. If he isn't on the platform delivering a speech in a highly characteristic style (which Don Rickles has tried to imitate, with pitiful results) he is somewhere in the crowd, dominating it by the sheer force of a seven-foot personality crammed into a—well, never mind his height. He denies it, anyway.

And if for some reason, Harlan is silent, that still doesn't matter. You can even have your back to him and be unaware that he is within five states of where you are standing, but from the way all the young ladies in the place are shaking, you know at once that that must be Harlan behind you somewhere and he may not even be doing anything.

Is this a Good Thing? Sure, it's a Good Thing. Those of us who want Science Fiction to be famous and highly regarded have to get it to the attention of all those Dumb People out there, and how are we going to do that? I can't. Here I stand, with a face like a Greek god and with writing ability without compare, and with the ability to write hundreds of books on hundreds of subjects, and I create only the slightest of ripples. (I'll kill you if you agree with me.)

Harlan, on the other hand, need only turn around and he creates a tidal wave.

Science fiction profits; at least people hear of it ("Oh, yeah, that's the stuff this crackpot Harlan Ellison writes!")

Besides, Harlan makes it possible for science fiction writers to get together. Without him, what is there to do? Two writers meet:

"Hello" "Hello" "How're things?" "Okay, I suppose. And you?" "Okay. Anything new?" "No, and you?" "No."

Deadly. Deadly.

As it is, though, the two writers meet, eyes glinting, lips trembling eagerly—

"Hello" "Hello, hey did you hear the latest about Harlan?" "No, what did he do now?" "Whisper, whisper, whisper." "NO! Do you know what I heard in that connection?" "No" "Whisper, whisper, whisper." "GOOD GOD, did he do that?"

The conversation continues for hours and the two writers are friends forever.

It's a great thing Harlan does, cementing friendship that way. So it's only right that there be a book of Ellison and that I contribute my bit to the evidence that he really *does* write stories. *That* rumor is correct.

—Isaac Asimov

THE
BOOK
ABOUT
ELLISON

ESSENCE OF ELLISON
Lee Hoffman

How can one begin to describe Harlan Ellison? To say that he is a human being is like saying that lightning is a meteorological phenomenon—it's true and elemental, but it is far from adequate. One might say that each is a brilliance that lights the field of vision, present long enough to impress the senses profoundly but gone from sight before one can completely focus on it. When I visualize Harlan, I imagine his face—sharp and intense—but trailing images of itself like those open shutter photographs of headlights on a highway at night. An impression of Harlan is not a static thing—motion is an essence of the subject. Motion and energy—one might start to describe him as pure energy compacted into human form.

Harlan first blazed across my field of vision nigh fifteen years ago at a Midwestcon. Engulfed in a cloud of pipe-smoke and a patter of monologues, he was a sharp-featured, quick-tongued young fan who could charm his audience and cut deep at his victims. Harlan made friends quickly in those days—and enemies equally quickly. He was outspoken and direct, opinionated and never afraid to speak his mind.

When I saw him at the Westercon this year, the haze of pipe-smoke was thinner, the patter of monologues more polished. Harlan charmed and entertained his audience with the skill of a professional. Still outspoken and direct, with a wit more fine-honed than ever, he is probably still as capable as ever of making quick enemies. He is still opinionated, still unafraid to speak out. But now his opinions are more considered and his arguments more matured. He has a lot to say—a lot which is well worth listening to.

Harlan is a seeker after truths. He storms battlements and attacks with such force that occasionally members of his audience are dazzled by the pyrotechnics and miss the points—the goals he's striving after. And then there are some members of the audience who still think of Harlan Ellison as the brash young fan he was almost a decade and a half ago—who know him only by an image which has been perpetuated through the wealth of Harlan Ellison Stories still in circulation. (Harlan himself tells these stories with masterful artistry.) To accept only a superficial and distorted image of Ellison—to shrug off his statements without consideration is not only unfortunate, it's intellectual blindness. One may not always agree with his conclusions, but the ideas deserve a damned lot of thought.

Harlan's speech at the Westercon banquet, where he was guest of honor, brought down the house. It was a masterpiece of speechmaking and in one way I feel sorry for those people who will only read the printed words without being able to see and hear Harlan himself. But on the other hand, making the speech, Harlan was also overwhelming his audience with the intensity of his own personality. It will be easier to give studied consideration to his ideas when reading the words than it was while listening to him speak them.

Despite his dazzling displays of humor, Harlan Ellison is an intensely serious young man. He has always written "from the gut." He lives the same way—with a depth and intensity of emotion. He *experiences* life and environment with the whole of himself. And from his very beginnings as a writer, he has struggled to express this depth of feeling in his work.

Financially, Harlan is a successful writer. Artistically, he's been acclaimed by readers, critics and fellow-writers. But yet, in a very important sense, he has not yet succeeded. He is still an experimenter with ideas, still a seeker within himself as well as in the world around him. And there is an essence of Ellison which is still untapped.

I feel that when the day comes that Harlan finds the way to express that essence in words, you're going to see the bright lightning of genius on the printed page.

—Lee Hoffman, July 1966

HARLAN ELLISON
Ted White

The 1957 Midwestcon was my first. I had been to two worldcons, and was a fairly active, well-known fan. But I was not too familiar with many of the fans who made up the Midwestcon Bunch at that time. So to some extent, I hovered on the fringes.

There was a big gag making the rounds. Harlan Ellison was in the Army, and someone had brought to the con a book about the Army. It was passed from hand to hand, and everyone signed the endpapers and scribbled a note. By the time the book got to me, it said things like, "Hey Harlan, *this'll* make a man out of you!" and "How'd a runt like you make it into the Army?", and "Where's my sub money to *Dimensions*, you bastard?" and other epitomes of wit and wisdom.

I joined in the game, scribbled an insult and my name, and passed it on to my neighbor.

I have regretted that, felt a deep embarrassment for it, ever since.

I first came into contact with Harlan in 1953. Early that

year, I'd drawn a cover for Joel Nydahl's *Vega,* and Joel, who was a flash-in-the-pan BNF, suggested to Harlan that he get in touch with me. Harlan was then publishing a fanzine called *Science Fantasy Bulletin;* it had previously been the *Cleveland Science Fantasy Bulletin,* a clubzine. By now it was averaging sixty to eighty pages an issue, and every page was crammed with art and material by most of the top names in fandom, and many name pros.

Harlan wrote me and asked if I'd care to illustrate some stories for *SFB.* I was flattered, and accepted. Later, he sent a story. I don't recall the author—it might have been Bert Hirschman—but it was concerned with space travel in some fashion. I did three or four wretched drawings in india ink (which I had no mastery over), and that was the last I was asked to do for *SFB.*

Time passed. *SFB* became *Dimensions,* and had two more issues, close to a year apart.

Then it was 1955, and the Clevention, my first con. I was with John Magnus, who was a buddy of Harlan's, so I tagged along as Harlan led a bunch of us to a department store to buy ties for Roger Sims, or maybe George Young, pausing on the way to give directions to a man working on a light pole, and causing a total commotion in the department store.

I had almost no opportunity to talk with Harlan during the con, but I managed to tag along on a number of occasions. At one point, we were walking down the stairs from the mezzanine together, and I told Harlan that I liked the way he dressed—I was only becoming conscious of good clothes then, and Harlan was as much then as now a sharp dresser. On another occasion Harlan was trying to sell a subscription to *Dimensions* to another fan. I was passing by, and he halted me, saying, "Here's Ted White. He'll tell you what a great fanzine *Dimensions* is. Is it worth subscribing to, Ted?"

"Sure," I said. "I'd sub to it if you weren't sending it to

me anyway. . ."

I'd brought a super-lightweight portable typer with me to the con. I was sharing a suite with John Magnus, Harlan, and the Detroit boys (I think I shared a bed with Fred Prophet, but my memory is a little dim now) and I recall Harlan shaking me awake to say, "Hey, that neat little portable of yours—wanta sell it?" He gave me some money down and said he'd send me the remaining amount later.

Next year it was the NYCon II. Harlan was married now, a selling writer, living on the upper west side in Manhattan. Several of us dropped over to visit him before the con. I didn't have much more chance to talk with him than before, although I did ask him about the money he owed me. He told me he'd have it for me shortly.

So when that book came to me, at the Midwestcon the following year, I wrote something like "Did you escape into the Army to avoid paying me?"

Harlan in the fifties cultivated kookiness. He did schticks, but in a more improvisational sense. He might be walking down the street, and suddenly stop us all, walk up to a total stranger, and lauuch into a schtick which convulsed us all in total helpless laughter, while the stranger grew more and more puzzled by this crazy man and his friends.

That was the on-stage Harlan, the Harlan on display in public. That was the Harlan who, at the 1958 Midwestcon, in driving us to the banquet, nearly caused the heart-failure of all his passengers with his insane driving, pausing in headlong flight to drive onto the sidewalk and corner a hapless pedestrian for directions, muttering, all the time, "We're late—I'm the toastmaster, and we're late . . ."

I was part of the Public, an admiring member of the audience of dull people who were enlivened by this energetic performer in our midst. I saw Harlan exclusively in his Public facet. I heard his explanation, with running dialogues, of how *Lowdown Magazine* had printed his picture as "Cheech Beldone," a juvie hood, and butchered his article. I watched with something close to awe, as he took command of a fancy expensive restaurant. Harlan was the Swinger in fandom. The Rest of us were Clods.

But not everyone appreciated this fact. Many were jealous of Harlan, and more were rubbed the wrong way by his mannerisms, his usurpation of the spotlights. When the subject of Harlan Ellison came up at parties, there were two kinds of Harlan Ellison stories that would be told. On the one hand, there were the funny things, the What-a-gassy-thing-happened-the-last-time-I-was-out-with-Harlan variety. But there were also the cruel ones, the ones about That Bastard Ellison, and How I Really Screwed Him Up, which, in the right company, would be greeted with howls of glee.

I never enjoyed those stories. An adolescent underdog myself, I didn't get much kick out of the stories of How I Shat On Harlan. I had as much reason as any of them to dislike Harlan—it was years before I got the rest of my money from him—but somehow I'd never been able to work up a good hate against him.

When Harlan moved back to New York in 1960, I was living here. And, to my surprise, he looked me up. As a matter of fact, he ended up staying in my apartment until he could find one for himself—one which turned out to be in the same block. He'd broken with his first wife, and turned his back on an editorial job with Bill Hamling in Chicago, and now he was back in NYC, freelancing.

It was in this period that I got to know Harlan as a person, to see him with his defenses down, the Private and real Harlan Ellison.

There were a few stormy moments between us. Harlan is such a totally volatile person that there had to be. But I will say this here and now: if I liked Harlan Ellison before—and then it could only have been the attraction of the glamor he attached to himself—I liked him better now. Harlan was a good friend. Although 3,000 miles separate us now, and we see each other infrequently, I would like to think that we remain good friends. Each of us was in the other's debt more than once, during the time Harlan lived in New York; we did a great deal together. We drove all over the city in Harlan's Austin-Healy—I was one of the few he would trust to drive it for him—we visited editorial offices together, took in concerts, jazz clubs, restaurants. It was an exciting period for me. And a valuable one. Harlan taught me a lot about writing, directly and indirectly, and was responsible for my first sale to *Rogue*.

It was during this period that the Affair of My Typewriter was resolved.

Harlan had never finished paying me. His problem was that he had enjoyed almost no use of the machine. He had taken it home with him from the Clevention, and almost as soon as he was back in NYC, Ken Beale had borrowed it. Ken hocked it, and lost the ticket. So Harlan had no typer, and no means to get it back.

1960 was the year of the PittCon, and also the year Eric Bentcliffe won TAFF and Joy and Sandy Sanderson left Inchmery and emigrated to the US—specifically, to the Bronx.

New York fandom got together to have a party for Eric on his arrival. Belle Dietz suggested it be at their place. When we all got to the party, it turned out to be more in honor of the Sandersons. And when Harlan got there, he found Ken Beale in attendance. Harlan spoke a few threatening words to Ken, suggesting that Ken pony up the money for the typewriter he had virtually stolen, so that Harlan could pass it along to me, whom he still owed.

Ken allowed as how it was all water five years uuder the bridge. Harlan, indignant at this cavalier attitude, and feeling guilty for having owed the money to me for so long, became angry, and suggested that Ken had better rethink things. He put it more strongly than that, actually.

He must've scared Ken, or at least impressed him. Ken told the story to Calvin Thomas Beck and Mama Beck, and the latter apparently acted true to form.

A few weeks later, on a Sunday afternoon, two cops from the narcotics squad raided Harlan's apartment.

Now Harlan's only vice is smoking. He does not drink, and his attitude toward drugs is actually puritanical. Harlan was badly shaken that he should be raided by the narcotics cops. To him their very presence was a slander against him. He volunteered to let them conduct a thorough search.

They found no narcotics, of course.

But they found something else. They found a box in which Harlan had a small, .22 revolver, a switchblade knife, and a set of brass knuckles. These had been tucked into a closet, and were souvenirs of the days when Harlan had pretended to be "Cheech Beldone," in the slums of Brooklyn.

They arrested Harlan for a violation of the Sullivan Act, the harsh New York State law on the possession of fire-arms and concealed weapons.

Harlan's mother was in town that weekend. Monday I drove her and Linda Soloman, a girl who lived in Harlan's building, down to the criminal courts building in Harlan's car. It was a rainy, gusty day. A hurricane was hitting New York City, the last one we've had. Theron Raines, Harlan's agent at that time, met us. This was the arraignment. The judge droned on in a bored voice, and without giving Harlan a word edgewise, set bail, and moved on to the next case.

Harlan was home the next day, on bail. He was shaken. The conditions in the jail, The Tombs, had disgusted and upset him, as well they might. He spent half an hour telling me about them, his voice tense and occasionally breaking. The strain had been a hard one.

"Harlan," I said, "You might as well try to get something out of this. Why don't you write it up for the *Village*

Voice?" He was then a contributor to the *Voice.* "Write it up, tell people about it. If you're outraged, this is one way to communicate it in a way that might do some real constructive good."

"You're right, Ted," he said.

A couple of weeks later, the *Voice* (a weekly) came out with a banner over the masthead: "BURIED IN THE TOMBS: HARLAN ELLISON."

The progression of events after that was steam-roller-like. The wire-services had run an item on Harlan's arrest; his doorman had tipped them off. Early versions made it sound like Harlan was a gun-running junkie. Various fans picked up the item and some of them made gleeful noises—boy, Harlan had sure gotten *his,* now!

The charge was eventually dismissed, but in the meantime Bill Hamling had seen the *Voice* piece. He wanted Harlan to do it over as a book. Harlan had remarried. He needed steady employment. That fall he and his wife moved back to Chicago, and Harlan launched the Regency Books line under Hamling. The sixth book released was the one the idea of which had been responsible for the line: *Memos from Purgatory* by Harlan Ellison.

On the back of the title page is a note: "NOTE: Brief passages from BOOK TWO: 'The Tombs' appeared in *The Village Voice* . . . as 'Buried in the Tombs,' and are used here in greatly expanded form."

But, on the facing page—"When the dark begins to close in around you, a friend can be identified by the candle he carries. *So this book is dedicated* To TED E. WHITE."

That's the first and only time a book has been dedicated to me. And as Harlan mentioned at the Westercon this year, "I don't dedicate books lightly, you know, Ted."

I appreciate that.

And, more important, I appreciate Harlan Ellison. To me it is less important what he is—be it science fiction writer, TV or movie scripter, or just a bombastic and dynamic fan—than who he is. Who he is is Harlan Ellison, a good and valuable friend.   —Ted White, 1966

THE JET-PROPELLED BIRDBATH

Robert Silverberg

I first met Harlan Ellison at the 1953 world SF convention, in Philadelphia. Our previous contacts had been by mail and telephone; but I spotted him almost the instant I had entered the Bellevue-Stratford Hotel. He was the little guy in the center of the crowd, doing all the talking and obviously holding the audience in the palm of his hand.

"Ellison?" I said. "Silverberg."

He said something snide, and a deep and strange friendship was born.

Two Ellison episodes of that 1953 convention stand out clearly. One took place on the final night, in the hotel lobby. A certain New York fringe fan named Joe Semenovich had taken offense at some remarks of Harlan's, and had come to the convention that Monday to "get" him, bringing along two anthropoid goons. The three hoods—as sinister-looking as you can imagine—converged on Harlan in the lobby. Any sensible man would have disappeared at once, or at least yelled for the nearest bell-hop to stop the slaughter. But Harlan stood his ground, snarled back at Semenovich nose-to-nose, and avoided mayhem through a display of sheer bravado. Which demonstrated one Ellison trait: physical courage to the verge of idiocy. Unlike many tough-talking types, Harlan is genuinely fearless.

The other episode occurred at the banquet of that convention. The toastmaster (Bloch? Asimov?) announced that Harlan and a quondam fan of great gifts named Dave Ish had sold a story to Tony Boucher's *F&SF*. A beaming Harlan confirmed the revelation: the story was called "Monkey Business," I think, and was 2500 words long, and the payment had been $100. As a fledgling neopro myself, I felt the tinge of admiration well mixed with envy. But the announcement was in error. Harlan and Dave hadn't quite sold "Monkey Business" yet; they had merely *submitted* it. In due time Boucher read it and rejected it. It had only seemed, to Harlan's eager imagination, that a story so good was certain to be sold. Which illustrates a second Ellison trait: a hunger for literary success so powerful that it dissolved the distinctions between fact and fantasy.

For a long time, Harlan's literary triumphs were of the same illusory order. In December 1953, he came to New York and visited me at Columbia, where I was then in my sophomore year. My roommate was out of town, and he stayed overnight with me. In a pizzeria on Amsterdam Avenue we discussed our future plans for professional success. In my case the future had already begun, for I had sold a couple of stories and even a novel. Harlan, too, had "sold" a novel: a 27,000 word juvenile called *Starstone*. Gnome Press was going to publish it, he told me proudly. Only it wasn't so. Harlan was anticipating reality again, and reality ultimately failed him.

He went back to Cleveland, and I didn't hear much from him for over a year. I pursued my writing career with indifferent success, scratching out a few sales to Bill Hamling and Bob Lowndes. In the Spring of 1955 Harlan reappeared in New York, this time to stay. He rented a room on the floor below mine, and set up a literary shop. I am still awed by the fastidiousness of his room. Everything was in its place, and stayed there. And everything was tasteful, down to a little leather hassock that I bought from him when he felt the pinch of cash, and that I keep in my office to this day. He took a job in a bookstore during the day, and wrote SF at night.

The summer of 1955 was a long, hot, brutal one for Harlan. He didn't sell a thing. There was the famous time when he reported that he had a crime story "90% sold" to *Manhunt*—for so an editor of that once-celebrated magazine had told him. But the editors of *Manhunt* were pseudonymous myths, the stories were bought en bloc from Scott Meredith, and Harlan's story was in the mailbox, rejected, the next day. Getting the last 10% of that sale had been too much.

A few weeks later he swaggered into my room and declared, "You'll be glad to know I hit Campbell today, Bob." I had visions of the towering JWC sagging to the floor of his office, blood spouting from his nose, while Harlan stood above him stomping his sinus-squirter into ruin. But no: all Harlan meant was that he had sold a story to Campbell. He hadn't, though.

So it went for him, one imaginary sale after another in a hellish summer of frustration and failure. That I was now selling stories at a nice clip did not improve Harlan's frame of mind, for our friendship always had a component of rivalry in it. When Randy Garrett came to town and moved into our building, he began collaborating not with Harlan the would-be writer, but with Silverberg, the successful new pro. The summer became a daze for Harlan; jeered at from all sides, he clung somehow to his goal and banged out an immense, bloated, preposterous novelette called "Crackpot Planet." He sent it off to *If,* and then went back to Cleveland to visit his family.

Now I had read most of Harlan's stories that summer, and

many of them seemed of full professional quality to me—one called "Life Hutch," another called "Glowworm." But "Crackpot Planet" struck me as a dog, and I told him so. He shrugged. A couple of weeks went by. Then I went to his mailbox downstairs to collect his day's mail and forward it to him, and there was a letter from *If*. They were buying "Crackpot Planet," all 17,000 absurd words of it.

It was not Harlan's first sale. Larry Shaw had bought "Glowworm" for his new *Infinity*, and an expose-magazine had picked up something by Harlan about kid-gang life. (But that's a story in itself, as Harlan will agree. Eh, Cheech?) But those two sales had been to friends of Harlan, and so perhaps were tainted by personal sympathies. The sale to *If* had been coldly professional: a story sent off to a strange editor, an acceptance coming back. Harlan was in.

There was no stopping him after that. By the end of 1956, he was selling at least a story a week, and in the succeeding ten years he's never had much difficulty persuading editors to buy his wares. His early work was awkward and raw—a weird compound of Nelson Algren and Lester del Rey, in which he managed to absorb the worst features of each, meld them, add liberal dollops of Hemingway, Walt Whitman, Ed Earl Repp, and Edgar Allan Poe, and top off with a wild melange of malapropisms. But there was a core of throbbing excitement within all that nonsense, and the inner power remained within him as the outer junk sloughed away with maturity.

For the last few years we've lived on opposite sides of the continent, keeping in touch fitfully. I regret that, because Harlan's recent successes in Hollywood and in science fiction have eliminated that residue of envy that often tinged our friendship in the 1950's. There are things I have that Harlan still covets, but professional success is no longer one of them. And, as he knows, there are some things for which I envy him. So old wounds are healed and old debts cancelled.

Not long ago I happened past 114th Street, where Harlan and Randy and I lived that blistering, tense summer twelve years ago. The place looks the same from the outside. I wonder how long it'll be before they put the commemorative plaque on the door. —Robert Silverberg, 1967

7000 MORE WORDS ABOUT HARLAN ELLISON

David Gerrold

Recently, I discovered something interesting about Harlan Ellison—or rather, his impact. I was working at Universal Studios for a while, and I was on the top floor of "The Tower" (a big black building where important decisions are supposed to be made) and while I was waiting for my appointment I began chatting with one of the secretaries. She asked me what I wrote, I told her mostly science fiction, and she asked, "Oh, do you know Harlan Ellison?" I paused before I answered. I did more than pause. I hesitated.

And while I was hesitating, I realized that I *was* hesitating. And then I realized that almost everybody hesitates when they are asked, "Do you know Harlan Ellison?"

The length of the hesitation is directly proportional to the length of time you have known Harlan Ellison. If you have only seen Harlan at a convention or one of his public appearances, then your hesitation will be so short ("Uh, yes—I've seen him.") as to be practically unnoticeable. If you've been to his house or gone to dinner with him, the pause is anywhere from one to three heartbeats before you answer. If you've known him six months, the pause may be several seconds. If you've known Harlan for a year or six, it is distinctly possible that your eyes will glaze over for a moment or two before you respond.

I've known Harlan Ellison for ten years.

It took me almost thirty seconds—my mouth went dry, palpitations afflicted my heart, a cold sweat broke out all over my body, all the usual symptoms—before I could manage to croak out, "I'm familiar with his work."

This phenomenon—the Harlan Ellison hesitation syndrome—as near as I have been able to determine, is universal: it afflicts publishers, editors, TV talk-show hosts, network vice-presidents, head-waiters, producers, and any officer of any union or association of which Harlan was ever once a member. It doesn't matter whether you have been close to Harlan or not, whether you have been his friend or enemy or both (yes, that's not only possible, it's mandatory).

It doesn't matter what the nature of the relationship was—if you have experienced personal contact with Harlan Ellison, then whenever anyone asks you, "Do you know Harlan Ellison?" your whole life will flash before your eyes before you can answer. The longer you've known him, the more life there is to flash, and the longer it takes before you can respond.

The reason for this is that knowing Harlan Ellison is like riding a roller coaster—not your fancy, flashy ones that ride on steel tubes and couldn't come off the track if you took a crowbar to it—but the old-fashioned rickety wooden kind that they don't build any more; the ones with crests so high you got a nosebleed just looking up to the top. The brightly painted superstructure, usually yellow or white with red trim, would sway visibly in a high wind—and your friends would whisper to you how just last week one of the cars came off the rails on Suicide Curve, the place where you weren't supposed to stand up in the car or you would go flying off into space, probably to impact in a special walled-off area (the amusement park owners had very carefully computed the trajectories of flying bodies) where no one could see and they could hush the whole thing up or the city would make them tear the roller coaster down—that's the kind of roller coaster Harlan Ellison is. There is serious doubt as to whether or not you will survive your encounter with it, and if you do, there is equal doubt as to whether you will retain enough of your gray matter to be capable of rational intercourse in the real world.

The reason for all of this expository material is that because Harlan Ellison is going to be the Guest of Honor at this year's Worldcon—Iguanacon in Phoenix, Arizona—there is going to be a great deal of material written about him before, during and after the event. It will appear in fanzines and prozines alike. We will see interviews, analyses, exposes, and personal profiles that will attempt to cover Harlan Ellison from every angle, top to bottom, inside and out.

I suspect that most of them will get it *wrong*.

Not intentionally, you understand—I'm certain that the people who will be writing about Harlan will be individuals of good will; but they will be attempting the impossible: they will be attempting to *explain* Harlan Ellison.

It would be easier to put a leash on a whirlwind.

The easy answer is that there are some things that the mind of mortal man was not meant to know. The internal dynamics of the entity called Harlan Ellison tend to fit into this category, defying all rational description, let alone coherent analysis.

This is not a casual opinion. While I am not a professional Harlan-watcher, in the ten years since I was first exposed to the man, I have watched him go through a variety of adventures and misadventures. One thing, at least, *is* certain—Harlan Ellison is a highly emotional entity—not only for himself, but for others as well. He lives his life in high gear—and like the speeding driver who barrels past the rest of us on the highway, he scares the hell out of us—we can't imagine that he actually has control over all that velocity. He does (I think)—that velocity is probably only a byproduct of the controlled fusion reaction that drives the man. If he can control the fusion reaction of his own emotions, he can certainly control where they are taking him. The problem is that too many of the rest of us, especially those with weak rudders, get caught up in his wake and are momentarily overwhelmed. The reactions range from wide-eyes wonder (like those who were touched by the UFO's in *Close Encounters*) to outright phobia (like Christopher Lee confronted by a crucifix).

More than once, I have met individuals who are prepared to tell me how great Harlan is—I never argue the point, but usually, their opinions are formed on the basis of only a brief acquaintanceship with Harlan—and usually their opinions are too shortsighted to recognize the complexity of the man. (These individuals often fade away after a little while more. . . .)

Individuals who have known Harlan for any length of time (five years or more) tend to be more cautious about what they say. Those of us who regard ourselves as Harlan's friends (and the list is constantly changing) have learned that Harlan Ellison's faults are as great as his virtues—but he's entitled to his faults, he comes by them honestly—you either learn to accept them or you keep your distance. The house rule at Ellison Wonderland is *"Dig. Or Split."*

What I want to do here is share an incident with you. No, I am not going to tell the story about Harlan and the waterbed salesman, nor the one about Harlan and the baby elephant, nor even the one about Harlan and the ambassador's daughter. Everybody knows those stories, and they've been told so many times that even people who weren't there when they happened can tell the stories better than those of us who were actual witnesses. No, instead, I'm going to tell you a story about Harlan that nobody knows but me.

A couple years back, Harlan and I had an argument. I don't remember exactly what it was about, but it was my turn to have the argument with Harlan, so I dutifully reported to the front line and had a fight with him. After a while, he got mad at someone else, so he and I made up. He mumfled and merfled something that several professional observers think might have been an apology for starting World War II, and I apologized for whatever sins I had been guilty of and promised to repair the shotgun holes in his kitchen wall.

But during that brief time (several millennia, I believe) that we had been angry with each other, I had been very very angry. I was so angry with Harlan Ellison that words almost failed me—almost, not quite. One afternoon, I sat down at my typewriter and wrote the following:

Sometimes he woke up in the middle of the night, in his own bed, and wondered where he was. The memories of a hundred different bedrooms fought and shifted—the question wasn't *where* so much as *who am I?*

When he finally did remember, it was almost always with pain.

He was a munchkin trapped in a land of Dorothies.

He had been dropped into the middle of Kansas and could not find his way back home. There were no friendly wizards here to take him, no good witches or yellow brick roads. And every time he tapped the heels of his red slippers together three times and said, "There's no place like home, there's no place like home—" he found himself back in Kansas, which was certainly no place like *home*. He couldn't get out—*he couldn't get out,* and after a while, frustration, rage and despair began to take its toll. Munchkins, of course, are the evolutionary source creatures for a host of

small magic and grotesque things: elves, gnomes, lepre-
chauns, but also in a darker sense, trolls, hobgoblins and evil
sprites. It's when they start to sour that they take the latter
direction, and that's what happened to this one.

Since the day he had *begun*—not born, just begun—
dropping from the sky in a dark tornado, he'd been a
savage, a barbarian at the center of his own universe, unable
to distinguish between *me* and *not-me,* and then later,
equally unable to discern the difference between *mine* and
not-mine. When he couldn't have something, he raged—his
anger was a firestorm, a roaring holocaust—and when the
universe resisted (as it usually did, impassive and detached),
his fires only smouldered, waiting for another chance; his
frustration fathered deeper anger and resentment.

His friends had named him—no, not his *friends,* for he
had none; just those who were close to him, because those
who were close to him could not stay his friends for
long—they called him The Little Monster. That he was
magic, there was no doubt, but that he was a malevolent
magic was also evident.

It was a hell of a life for a munchkin.

He couldn't get out. So he got even.

He studied the magic of the land of Dorothies, studied it
hard, and learning some of its secrets, he knew just enough
to be dangerous. He learned the magic of the language, the
symbols of manipulation—he practiced and grew skilled. He
mastered what he could and turned those spells against the
inhabitants of Dorothyland, those mundanes who, by their
plastic-scuttlefish existence, gave him so much pain; he
blamed *them* for his entrapment here in Kansas-colored
prison. So he cast his appropriated spells over all who fell
within his reach. He built gaudy, grotesque brocades of
alphabet and grammar; he tangled with the warp and woof
of concept, and fashioned baroque and rococo structures of
impossible events, ensnaring and enchanting with a madden-
ing logic of their own, sentence knotting around sentence,

gingerbread paragraphs towering one upon another; he piled them ever higher and wound his listeners ever deeper into his control. Just as he manipulated words, The Little Monster manipulated people with them. He grew as contemptuous of them as he was of the language, because he used his words too easily.

He strung together words like pretty beads upon a string, not so much for what they said or the way that they related to each other, but for the particular glisten and sparkle that each individual bead had, hoping that the whole effect of the whole string of beads would be one grand and glorious sparkle. Sometimes it was. Sometimes The Little Monster really was brilliant, in a way. More often he devalued the very magic he depended on. More often it was a clashing, crashing gaudiness which entranced the unwary, but only thundered at those who still knew something of delicacy—

—when he met those kinds of people, he only increased his efforts—if he couldn't dazzle them with one string of pretty beads, he'd try to blind them with a hailstorm of fire, and if that failed too, he'd tie them up in all the strands and leave them gasping—

Even so, there was a quality about the words he used and the thoughts embedded in them, a vitality, a power, a feigned ingenuousness that tantalized and caught even the most skeptical and jaded. He knew how to overwhelm the sensibilities—it was his *real* magic working—not his appropriated craft, but his innate munchkin skill, twisted, bent, bizarre, but magic nonetheless.

Eventually, or perhaps inevitably, he linked up with a typewriter, it being some*one* or *-thing* that he could talk to who could not walk away. *A typewriter can't reject you.* The pattern of his life was to reject others before they could have a chance to reject him; but a typewriter *couldn't*—a typewriter is the greatest friend ever invented for lonely people. It is the perfect conversationalist because it only listens, it never talks back, it never interrupts—although there *was* a point in The Little Monster's life when his typewriter had been possessed by an evil spirit and had in fact rejected him, which was such a shock to his psyche that he went into a writer's block for more than a year; he never cured it, he only learned to live with it—raging at it furiously, he treated it as one more obstacle that this ugly-gray-Kansas-universe kept dropping on him, the work of the same malevolent tornado that had ripped him from the technicolor world where he belonged. He worked despite the block, as he worked despite his chronic heartburn and his fourth divorce. He wrote roughshod over all these obstacles. He trampled the writing block under hobnailed sentences, as if it were the Third Reich and he was an avenging Yahweh, an angry Judaic God of thuggery and self-righteousness, an elemental force of havocked nature, a moral juggernaut avenging an eternal wrong—he did not solve his crises, he savaged them; he attacked not their roots, but their effects, and in the end, if he did not conquer, at least he *outlived.*

The Little Monster poured out words in a torrent of abuse. He was punishing the language for being so manipulatable. He respected only hard intransigence. He didn't love the language, that mutable tool, as did so many other writers; he used it as his slave to accomplish lower goals, a slave that had to be whipped in public every day, because he knew no other way to master it, no way to buy it, persuade it, gentle it or love it.

The Little Monster poured his bitterness and anger into his machine, and it listened well, and reported that bitterness and anger to a hundred million listeners, who were shocked and horrified, but too morbidly prurient to turn away from The Little Monster's bath of acid-prose scream of consciousness. That typewriter was plugged into amplifiers of a dozen different kinds: radios, records, movies, television sets, newspapers, magazines, anthologies, books—oh, the books! A flood of books, a maelstrom of raging words! Forests died for The Little Monster's anger.

And the brilliance—oh, the glarey-glarey brightness of it all! A savage fire in a land of vampire-Dorothies, blinding all who looked upon it with the naked eye and shriveling those who dared to approach too close. Except it wasn't really brilliance—

—not the real kind. It looked like brilliance, shone like it, because The Little Monster was *compulsively* brilliant—he wasn't brilliant in and of himself, he just edited out all the parts that didn't shine. He refused to recognize the parts of him that were tasteless, refused to let them exist; he would not let a tasteless thought or move or gesture express itself through him; so like a sculptor, he carved away everything from his life that didn't look like genius and thought the result actually was a work of genius, when in fact it was only the portrait of one—like Frankenstein's monster lying on the table, waiting for the spark of life, it was inanimate, an empty body, only the carcass of a genius—it moved like one, but it wasn't; it had never had a thought, never had a concept that wasn't a synthesis of all the other concepts it had previously encountered, never had a *new* perception of the universe. It merely reported things to people that they had not known before, but never things that were *un*known —it never once changed the thinking of the people who lived around The Little Monster, except to infect them with despair and bitterness. It was a device that synthesized pain, repackaged it in enticing new bottles—but it was still *old* pain—and made it look and move and talk like it had brilliance, and called that genius. His genius, if in fact it really was, was for *imitating genius;* but it worked, he fooled all the Dorothies, and he made them believe, and they turned back to him and pointed and said, "Yes, that *is* a genius." He hated them for being gulled, he was contemptuous of them; but still he gloried in their praise—it was the only praise he got—so he kept on carving at his writhing sculpture, portrait of his brilliance. Most of those who gazed upon it were startled by its glare, they shielded their eyes, thinking in that moment that they had actually been touched by brilliance—but the glare was only the anger of the process, not the brilliance of its product.

When they asked him why he could not write more cheerful stories, more optimistic ones—the kind of stories he characterized as "soft pink-and-white bunny rabbit stories," he only smiled with those sharpened teeth of his, and said, "I don't write for children. I tell stories of the real world, and the real world is full of pain—do you realize how much pain there is in the world?!!" It sounded profound. Hell, it sounded *empathic*. It sounded like a man *concerned*.

It was all part of his spell.

He didn't know how much pain there was in the world and he didn't care either—his job was only to survive Kansas. "There will always be pain, there will always be Kansas; there will only be *me* for a short while." He transcended all that Kansas heaped upon him, and he cherished that transcendence—he gloried in his own ability to dance circles around a crowd, dazzling them with pirouettes and fireworks and glorious thundering noises. Other people's pain only got between him and his audience, so he ignored it. If it wasn't his pain that he savaged his listeners with, then it would be other pains, borrowed ones and distant, but never with the audience's own, for that would make *them* the focus of attention, not himself—it had to be *his* and it had to be *he*, The Little Monster, who did the savaging; he would not turn that particular joy over to another—he guarded it as a private special pleasure of his own; his act of getting even with the uncaring corn-belt state.

The Little Monster lived in a tower. It was the only way he could look down on other men. Every year he had the tower raised a little higher, thus separating himself even farther and farther from the rest of the world. He imagined that the height which was the tower's was actually his own.

He prided himself on his height and his strength and his brilliance. But on those nights when he awoke not knowing where he was, he went prowling through the corridors, listening for the scrabbling of tiny claws. There were rats living in the walls of the tower and he fed upon them late at night when the moon was hidden behind the clouds.

—I *told* you I was angry. I was *very very* angry.

I wrote it as a therapeutic exercise. I had to get rid of all that anger somehow, and I wasn't going to vent it directly onto Harlan, so I poured it into my typewriter into the most deliberately ruthless look at Harlan that I could write.

I was very pleased with the nastiness in "The Little Monster." I really enjoyed writing it—it was *fun* being that angry. After a couple days of chortling about how clever I thought I had been, I finally put "The Little Monster" into a drawer and forgot about it. My anger had been burned off in the writing of it, and now I could return to the serious business of being a kind, gentle and compassionate person. The important thing was that I should deal with my own anger privately without adding to anyone else's pain in any way; that meant that the writing I had done had to remain private and forgotten. "The Little Monster" was my personal way of being angry for a while; it meant nothing more than a way to express a bit of nastiness without hurting anyone.

For two years now, "The Little Monster" has languished unread. I had forgotten about it, rediscovering the piece only recently while I was cleaning out my files. I reread it with amusement and amazement. "Gosh, I really was angry, wasn't I?" I said to the soon-to-be-world-famous Diane Duane, who works with me sometimes. "It's a pity that I can't share this with anyone though."

Of course, the word *can't* is a challenge. With the proper remarks to frame the piece, I *can* share it.

You see, my purpose here is not to honor Harlan Ellison the legend, but Harlan Ellison the human being—but to do that, first I *have* to deal with the legend. First I have to dismantle some of the nonsense that other people have surrounded the man with.

You see, "The Little Monster" is an evocation of the Harlan that people love to hate. There is, in science fiction circles, a kind of devil-worship surrounding the man—there are individuals who have, in their own minds, set him up as some kind of a demon who represents all that is terrible and wrong with whatever part of the world annoys them the most. To be sure, Harlan has never run from a confrontation, and oftentimes his opinions *are* controversial, but there are people who project onto him their own fears and frustrations and then blame him as the source. They honor him not with their praise, but with their hatred—which in a way is just another form of their *caring.* They express themselves in cheap shots and ridicule and contempt behind his back, if not for his work, then for his personality—they act as if Harlan Ellison is "science fiction's burden." They call him an *enfant terrible,* even though he is only six years shy of fifty, and looking forward to it. And when Harlan, in his never-ending battle to make us live up to the ideals to which we pay lip-service, confronts us with these truths, these people see it only as confirmation of what they already believe, because they cannot step away from their own blind attitudes to see where Harlan's anger is truly coming from. They see the rage and not the compassion. They've built an ugly legend around him because the legend is easier to deal with.

At the time I wrote "The Little Monster," I was serving that same shadowman image of him too—except that once I had gotten it out of my system, I didn't have to use it to bring pain to a man I still cared about very much; what I wanted was to stop hating him so I could like him again. I am printing the piece here because I want to drag that false image out into the open and hold it up to the light and show what a terrible burden some of us have inflicted on a very good man.

Most of the "facts" in "The Little Monster" are *not* true—they are deliberate misinterpretations in the service of a momentary anger—but the mood of the piece is true to some people; it is a reflection of what they believe, even if they cannot verbalize it as vividly. Harlan has become the man they love to hate. To many people, he really is The Little Monster—that is the subtext that is at work in the science fiction community. The Little Monster is the shadow-image of Harlan that fans will honor in the absence of the real Harlan—and they cannot and will not understand that as long as they *want* to see that image in Harlan, then that's what they will see, and no amount of protestations to the contrary will convince them of anything but what they already believe.

For instance, Harlan's "bad manners" are legendary— what most of the fans don't realize is that the "bad manners" are a defense against the colossal rudeness of some people who don't know how to act with courtesy. Harlan is a *genius* in his own right. He thinks faster and sharper than ninety per cent of the people around him; he is bored with banality, intolerant of pretentiousness, and deliberately hostile to stupidity in the hope that it will leave him alone. He justifiably detests jokes about his height because he has heard them all, and they're not funny any more, if they ever were. Isaac Asimov might be able to come up with a clever line about Harlan being short, and even Harlan will laugh—but Joe Neofan fresh off the street is *not* Isaac Asimov, never will be, and has not one tenth the cleverness necessary to come up with a line about short people that will rise above tastelessness. The odds are against it. The last person who did it well was Randy Newman, who wrote a song called "Short People," and even he called Harlan to apologize the day the album was released. So, can you blame the man for being annoyed when people he's never met are deliberately rude to him? He's heard those jokes before; he'd much prefer to be treated with courtesy—wouldn't we all?

(Besides, the truth of the matter is that Harlan is of normal height—most of the rest of us are abnormally tall. That's not a joke—the average height of the human race has been five foot six *or less* throughout recorded history; only recently have improvements in diet encouraged additional spurts of growth during adolescence, and it is only since the 1950's that we have begun to see a generation of six-footers.)

Those things are distractions—annoyances that only get in the way of the more important things that Harlan has to do on this Earth—he hates people who waste his time; that's why he's rude to them, so they'll go away. They are "persons from Porlock" who only want to keep him from his typewriter, who only want to steal his emotional energy for themselves, like selfish gluttons at a banquet.

"The Little Monster" is finally seeing print here only because Harlan has given his permission—I wanted to print it to demonstrate just how much it's possible to hate Harlan when you get angry at him. It will help me make the point.

You see, no matter how angry I get at Harlan, I cannot maintain that anger for long; because he did something for me once that was very important. I have never forgotten it—it was only a tiny act of kindness on his part, but at the time it happened it was the most important thing that anyone could have said or done. I have never forgotten that moment, and no matter what other fights Harlan and I may have in the future, they will only be temporary disturbances to me, because that one kind moment of Harlan's will redeem even the worst of his faults in my eyes.

You see, in 1969, I had a friend who I was very close to—perhaps the best friend I have ever had in my life; we were closer than brothers. At that time, I was still only a beginning writer and not very successful—Steve's friendship and support were very necessary to help me keep going because he believed in my ability; there were moments when it seemed as if he were the only one.

Steve was killed in a horrible and bizarre circumstance that defied rationality. I'm not going to go into detail here, I'm finally putting the story into a book to be called *Footnote**; but I was near-mad with grief, despair and loneliness, because I thought I had lost the one person in the world whom I could talk to. I was receiving very little comfort or compassion from individuals who were supposed to be my friends, and I was in a great deal of pain.

Finally, one afternoon, because I could not think of anyone else to call, I called Harlan.

At that time, Harlan and I were not friends, we were barely even acquaintances. We had met once or twice at conventions and that was the limit of it. Harlan had probably dismissed me in his own mind as a lucky kid who'd sold a script to a TV show he wasn't very fond of, but not much of a writer otherwise. I hadn't yet proved that I could put two words together to make a readable phrase, let alone a sentence, paragraph or coherent thought.

On the other hand, to me, Harlan embodied much of what I thought I wanted to be. He was successful, he was respected, and best of all, he seemed to have his act together.

So I called him and asked for help. *Real* help.

I suppose I caught him off balance. People don't normally ask other people for help, but I didn't know what else to do, and it seemed to me that if anyone knew what I could do, it would be Harlan.

He didn't really offer me any concrete suggestions—in fact, I don't remember very much of what was said—but what was said wasn't as important as the fact that Harlan took the time to talk to me, quietly and compassionately. He offered comfort. It doesn't sound like much, perhaps, but at that time, there was no one else I knew who was willing to take the time even to do that much. Harlan Ellison, who was probably "too important" to take time for one of the common people, proved that he was much more important than "too important." He probably had a lot of other obligations that demanded his attention, but he still took the time to try to help.

It wasn't *what* he said that helped. It was the fact that he cared enough to take the time.

All I have to do is remember that phone call, and I know that Harlan Ellison is no "Little Monster." He is a very big man—and those who characterize him otherwise, do a disservice not only to him, but to themselves as well, because they are holding themselves apart from someone who can *care* if only they would let him.

But perhaps we all prefer to hear the bad news first, because it's more exciting. If there is any truth to the image of Harlan as "The Little Monster," it is only half-truth; because if munchkins can go sour, they can also be sweet if you give them the chance to be. . . .

Harlan has probably forgotten all about that phone call. In the nine years since, we have both changed and grown a lot—something that fans aren't always quick to realize—we have had our share of differences, but if Harlan has never understood why I have insisted on remaining a loyal friend despite those differences, the reason is that he was willing to be a friend to me when I thought I had none, and I will do no less in return.

This piece has been a very personal one, and I decided to write it only after a great deal of thought—but if it helps to put a stake through the heart of The Little Monster shadowman, then it is worth the telling, because Harlan Ellison deserves a lot better than to be characterized as a mad munchkin.

It is time we began.

HARLAN ELLISON AND THE FORMULA STORY

Joseph Patrouch Jr.

Harlan Ellison has been writing science fiction since the mid-fifties. His writing has not stayed the same: several interesting developments have occurred in it. For example, his early SF features all the usual paraphernalia of conventional SF: robots, ray guns, spaceships, interstellar war, aliens. But all this was merely the lubricant which allowed him to penetrate the dry SF field and begin to function smoothly in it. Once he got his own stroke going, he didn't need that conventional imagery so much and so he largely abandoned it.

For me, SF is distinguished from other forms of fiction by its emphasis on "scientifically plausible alternate settings for consciousness." The farther one gets from scientific plausibility, the closer one gets to fantasy. During his career Ellison has evolved from SF writer to fantasist. In fact, even in many of his best-known SF stories he is as much fantasist as SF writer. Both " 'Repent, Harlequin!' Said the Ticktockman" and "I Have No Mouth and I Must Scream" employ time-honored SF conventions: the first concerns the dissenter in a technological "utopia," and the second the gigantic, nearly omniscient computer. In "Repent, Harlequin" Ellison conjures up a technological gimmick called a "cardioplate." When the Authorities erase a cardioplate, its owner has a heart attack and dies. This is a nice piece of SF furniture. But where most SF writers either would try to render such a gimmick plausible by explaining "scientifically" how it works or would avoid mentioning a rationale at all so as not to call attention to it, Ellison brazens it out by telling us "this simple scientific expedient utilize[s] a scientific process held dearly secret by the Ticktockman's office"! In other words, the rationale exists, but it isn't available to the writer. Similarly, in "Mouth/Scream" the war computers of the world unite, destroy all but five members of the human race, and keep them alive to torment and thus wreak its revenge on its creators. Along the way one of the captive survivors tries to escape: "Then he began to howl, as the sound coming from his eyes [?] grew louder . . . . The light was now pulsing out of his eyes in two great round beams. . . . His eyes were two soft, moist pools of pus-like jelly." One trained in reading SF instantly wonders, "What was the mechanism? How can the ability of a computer to liquefy eyes be rendered plausible?" But Ellison doesn't care. He never offers a rationale. The point: even in his most SF-like stories, Ellison is not concerned with scientific plausibility. He is basically a fantasist. Ellison is an SF writer by virtue of some of the furniture which he uses in his stories, by virtue of the markets to which he sells, and by virtue of the Hugo and Nebula awards which he accepts, but he is not an SF writer by virtue of his literary techniques. If you will, he is an SF writer by milieu, rather than by product.

The development which interests me most, however, since I tend to be a structuralist in my approach to fiction, is his evolution from the formula story to the experimental story, from the closed to the open, from the plotted to the unplotted. Let's examine some of Ellison's fiction in detail in order to see this development taking place.

"Life Hutch" was Ellison's second professionally published story (April 1956). It is set in the far-distant future during an interstellar war between Earth and Kyba. Life hutches—refuges where disabled men can await rescue after battle—have been established. The story is organized in the standard 1-2-3 pattern of the formula: 1) the narrative hook, or grabber, in which we see the hero in trouble; 2) the exposition, or the past of the story, in which we learn how the hero came to be in that trouble; and 3) the struggle and final victory in which the hero gets out of trouble. The grabber is only a page long. The central character, Terrence, is trapped in a life hutch, injured and dying, with a malfunctioning robot that will kill him if he moves. The exposition is given in a three-and-a-half page flashback marked at the start by "He let his eyes close completely, let the sounds of the life hutch fade from around him" and at the end by "The reliving of his last three days brought back reality sharply." In this flashback we are told about the Earth-Kyba war, about life hutches, about how Terrence came to be in that particular life hutch. Perhaps a trifle awkwardly, the major complication in the story—the point at which the central character is presented with the problem which he must solve in the rest of the story—is given, not in the narrative hook, but here in the flashback: "It was at this point that the service robot . . . had moved clankingly across the floor and with one fearful smash of a steel arm thrown Terrence across the room," breaking three of his ribs and putting him in the situation in which we found him when the story began. Problem: how to stay alive when any movement causes the robot to smash whatever moved?

In true SF fashion, the third part of the story has Terrence collect and analyze data. Key datum #1: the robot's "brain" is far too large to be kept in its moveable body and so it is stored in the wall from where it communicates with its body by radio. Key datum #2: Terrence has a flashlight on his belt. With this data Terrence can solve his problem. Can you, gentle reader? (One minor variation from the formula: Terrence "gets" the solution before we readers are told about the flashlight. Strictly speaking, the reader should be given all the data so he and the hero have a chance to figure out the solution together.)

The third part of the story ends with the climactic scene in which Terrence puts his solution into effect. (If that solution were not obvious from the hero's activities, then the story would require a concluding scene in which the problem-solver could explain how he figured it all out. In "Life Hutch" the solution is obvious, and no such concluding scene is necessary.) Terrence flashes his light on-and-off on the wall behind which is the robot's brain. The robot perceives the flashing as motion, walks over, and smashes in its own brain. Terrence of course lives happily ever after.

Except perhaps for putting the complication in the flashback and for having the hero solve the problem before giving the reader all the necessary clues to solve it himself, "Life Hutch" is a perfect little formula story. Note also, by the way, that this early Ellison story, besides having the formula problem-solving hero and the formula beginning-middle-end organization, also features a robot, spaceships, an interstellar war, aliens, and a ray gun—well, a flashlight. The point is that even in his second story Ellison was adept at using both the SF formula and the SF furniture. In fact, one feels that he would not have broken in to the field had he not been able to write this way. It was expected.

A second example of Ellison's use of the formula story seems in order. "Blind Lightning" was his third published SF story (June 1956). Like "Life Hutch" it is very carefully plotted. Like "Life Hutch" its basic pattern is 1) hero in trouble, 2) how the hero got in trouble, and 3) how the hero got out of trouble. But "Blind Lightning" is much more complex than "Life Hutch" because it has two narrative point of view characters instead of one and because it has three complications and resolutions instead of one.

The two characters are a human being named Kettridge and a telepathic, nine-foot-tall gorilla-Brahma bull-Kodiak bear of an alien named Lad-nar. Basically, "Blind Lightning" is Kettridge's story and best analyzed from his point of view. The opening sentence of the story describes the complication around which the story is built and puts both its characters before us doing something: "When Kettridge bent over to pick up the scurrying red lizard, the thing that had been waiting [Lad-nar] struck." Lad-nar takes the terrified and fainting Kettridge to his cave for use as food. Kettridge's immediate problem is obvious: like Ulysses in the cave of Polyphemous, he must remain alive and escape. The story is built around this problem.

But it is a more complex story than that. As part of the explanation of how Kettridge got into this trouble—i.e., as part of the exposition—we learn that years before Kettridge had shared the responsibility for the deaths of over twenty thousand people and that he is carrying that guilt around with him. Thus he has a secondary problem: he seeks a way to remove that guilt.

In the exposition of the story we also learn Lad-nar's background and problem: he and his intelligent kind are at the mercy of the lightning that becomes especially severe at certain seasons of that planet's year. The lightning has prevented a civilization from developing among these intelligent aliens. Lad-nar's—and his race's—problem is how to defeat/control/avoid the lightning.

Given these three complications, Kettridge is able to find a common solution: he can save his life, he can save his soul/reputation, and he can save Lad-nar's people all at once. As Ellison puts it:

> Here was a chance not only to survive [problem
> #1] but a chance to reinstate himself [problem

> #2] . . . . Ben Kettridge devised a plan to save his
> soul. . . . Lad-nar suddenly became a symbol of
> all the people who had been lost in the Mass
> Death. . . . He must save the poor hulk before
> him [problem #3]. And in saving the animal, he
> would save himself [problems #1 and 2].

Kettridge's solution is to have Lad-nar walk among the
lightning bolts wearing Kettridge's stretchable "insulating
metal-plastic." Kettridge goes out first, demonstrating the
safety of the suit. Then Lad-nar goes out—and returns alive.
All that remains is contact with Earth so that more suits can
be obtained.

Unfortunately, having saved himself from being eaten,
having removed the guilt from his soul, and having saved
Lad-nar's people from subservience to the lightning, Kettridge carelessly steps unprotected from the cave when his
fellow humans come to pick him up, lightning strikes him,
and he is killed. But his death strikes the reader, not as an
ultimate failure, but as a ratification and ennobling of what
he has done. Throughout the story Kettridge has reacted as
a human being rather than as the logical SF hero: he has
been afraid of the alien, he has fainted in the face of that
fear. Now, at the end, he is so relieved at the appearance of
other people that he forgets, is careless, and it costs him his
demonstrably human life. He is an emotional person. This
jars somewhat with the other major element in him and in
the story, the standard SF theme of "reason, reason uber
alles." Trapped in Lad-nar's cave, Kettridge "ran the whole
thing through his mind, sifting the facts, gauging the
information, calculating the outcome." Or, more succinctly,
"Only in his wits was there salvation." Kettridge is both
emotional *and* rational. For Ellison it is not either/or but
both/and.

Both "Life Hutch" and "Blind Lightning" clearly demonstrate that from the beginning of his writing career Ellison
knew and could manipulate the formula story. What is

interesting is that he wasn't content to write this kind of story for the rest of his career. As babies eventually outgrow their formula food, so Ellison outgrew the formula plot.

We have already seen Ellison bending the formula just a bit in a variety of ways. In "Life Hutch" he put the complication in the exposition instead of in the narrative hook and he had the hero solve the problem before he gave the reader all the necessary data. In "Blind Lightning" his hero faints with fear and is killed at the story's end instead of being always in control of himself and living happily ever after. And his refusal to explain the cardioplate in "Repent, Harlequin" or the eye-dissolving powers of the computer in "Mouth/Scream" can be cited as further examples of his refusal to play the game by formula.

In addition, I would like to instance an early story called "The Discarded" (April 1959). The formula requires a strong central character through whose actions and perceptions the reader can experience the story. The story is focused onto us through that central, narrative-point-of-view character. It is his story. This was certainly true of "Life Hutch," which has the traditional opening sentence in which the subject is the hero's name and the verb has that hero actively doing something: "Terrence slid . . ." are the first two words. "Blind Lightning" broke with this part of the formula a bit by putting us sometimes into the mind of Lad-nar instead of concentrating solely on Kettridge. "The Discarded" begins, "Bedzyk saw. . . ." Therefore, Bedzyk is the central character and the story will be organized around his perceptions as he solves some problem, right? Well. . . . Four pages from the end of the story Bedzyk is ray-gunned (this is still early Ellison, remember): "Bedzyk mewed in agony, and crumpled onto the deck. A huge hole had been seared through his huge chest. Huge chest, huge death." *Now* who is the story about? You can't kill off your narrative-point-of-view character. It just isn't done. It ruins the unity of the story. Since the reader has been identifying with this character, it's like killing off the reader, and that's too unsettling. And yet there's that Ellison at his typewriter, imagining the reader's discomfiture, and chortling, "Gotcha!" He knew the rules well enough to break them to get his desired effect.

Still, Ellison isn't known for those hundreds of formula and slightly-bent formula stories produced during his first years of writing. Certainly, many of those early stories contain passages that anticipate the writing style most often associated with him. That first sentence of "The Discarded," for example, continued, "Bedzyk saw Riila go mad, and watched her throw herself against the lucite port, till her pinhead was a red blotch of pulped flesh and blood." As Joanna Russ once remarked, "Ellison's mode is hyperbole." and this mode can be found often in Ellison's early work.

But it is not Ellison's style but his structure that I want to continue examining here. In the early and middle sixties he produced very few short stories of any kind, much less SF. He was busy writing TV scripts. One wonders about the extent to which his working in television influenced his later writing of fiction. What we view on the screen as a neat beginning-middle-end formula story is a rearrangement into chronological order of a mass of pieces created in a chaotic, disorganized sequence. A film viewed in the process of creation, rather than as a finished product, would have a curious, non-structured, non-chronological life of its own.

" 'Repent, Harlequin!' Said the Ticktockman" (December 1965) may be considered Ellison's "breakthrough" story (as "Nightfall" was for Isaac Asimov, "Neutron Star" for Larry Niven, and "The Doors of His Face, the Lamps of His Mouth" for Roger Zelazny). "Repent, Harlequin" took both the Hugo and the Nebula for its year, and Ellison has been an established SF writer ever since.

Two things about "Repent, Harlequin" especially interest me. First, in the light of my speculation above about the influence, on Ellison's sense of structure, of his experience in creating filmed stories, note that "Repent, Harlequin" is a non-chronological story. As the speaking voice says, "Begin in the middle, and later learn the beginning; the end will take care of itself." This structure is distantly related to that of "Life Hutch" and "Blind Lightning": narrative hook (man in situation), exposition (how did he get in?), struggle and victory (how does he get out?). The pattern of the formula story is dimly discernible in "Repent, Harlequin," but Ellison is not being non-chronological in the formula way. Instead, he has taken these pieces and put them in this order because they feel better to him. And the reader's own experience shows that Ellison was right: read the story in its beginning-middle-end sequence and see how much of its impact it loses. Despite its superficial resemblance to the formula story, "Repent, Harlequin" actually shows us Ellison growing out of the formula.

A second interesting thing about the story is the way Ellison interposes himself—or at least a speaking voice; for the sake of convenience, let's call it Ellison—between the story and the reader. The story is unified, not so much by its non-chronologically arranged series of events, as by the commentary and personality of Ellison the interlocutor. I take this as an early example of an Ellison story unified by the imposition of the author's personality, by an act of creative *will,* rather than by a cause-and-effect related series of external events called the plot or storyline.

"I Have No Mouth and I Must Scream" (March 1967) is very much like "The Discarded" and "Repent, Harlequin" in showing us the formula story receding in importance, but still there. In fact, examined closely, with an eye to its structure rather than its pyrotechnical style, "Mouth/Scream" is a fairly conventional story.

It begins with a narrative hook:

> Limp, the body of Gorrister hung from the pink
> palette; unsupported—hanging high above us in

the computer chamber; and it did not shiver in the chill, oily breeze that blew eternally through the main cavern. The body hung head down, attached to the underside of the palette by the sole of its right foot. It had been drained of blood through a precise incision made from ear to ear under the lantern jaw. There was no blood on the reflective surface of the metal floor.

Then Gorrister rejoins the group and they realize they've been tricked again, as they have been so often in the one-hundred and nine years they've been trapped inside the computer AM. Their problem is how to escape the torments of AM. Gorrister is one of a group of five who are kept alive to be the recipients of AM's fury. One of the other four, the I-narrator, Ted, is the narrative-point-of-view character.

From this narrative hook, we move to the exposition. Ellison does this in two rather conventional ways. First, the characters lecture the background at one another so the readers can overhear it. Ellison tries to make this plausible by making one of the characters insane and one of the marks of his insanity is his desire to hear the old story of the origins of AM and the destruction of humanity over and over again despite the fact that they all know it already. The readers, of course, don't, and so we get background via expository conversation. Ellison's second method for giving us the past of the story is having his point of view character, I=Ted, engage in interior monologues about his four companions—their pasts, the ways AM changed them when it captured them, their present personalities.

Then we get the struggle and victory. In the climactic scene, in which the hero puts his solution into effect, Ted murders two of his four companions while the third is murdering the fourth; then Ted murders the third, leaving himself the only one of the five still alive. For the sake of the story we must believe that all this happens so quickly that the nearly omniscient/omnipotent AM has no time to interfere. To prevent Ted's ever escaping too, AM turns him into "a great soft jelly thing" which has no mouth and must scream.

Narrative hook, activity in present interspersed with exposition, climactic scene and resolution, all presented through the thoughts and actions of a single character—how conventionally structured can a story be? Granted, Ted—like Kettridge, Bedzyk, and the Harlequin, but unlike Terrence—doesn't win and live happily ever after. But there are a lot more elements to a formula story than the happy ending, and "Mouth/Scream" has most of these other elements.

Three more things about the story. First, at its end all human beings but Ted are dead and gone, and Ted has been changed into that sentient lump of jelly. Ted has been recounting the events from his own present, when he is alone, jellied, with no hope. To whom is he addressing the words of the story, and in what medium? He has no mouth, so he can't be dictating it; he has no hands, so he can't be writing or typing; he has no audience, so he can't intend his account for anyone. What is the dramatic context of the words in the story?

Second, the I-narrator of "Mouth/Scream" is certainly put upon by a world he never made. And he is clearly paranoid about it. Of himself he insists, "I was the only one still sane and whole" while of his companions he says, "Those scum, all four of them, they were lined and arrayed against me. . . . They hated me. They were surely against me." Ted is an outstanding example of one of Ellison's typical narrative stances: it's me versus them, baby.

Finally, the theme of the story is clearly an important one. AM is symbolic of the technological world in which we all live and by which we are all, to one degree or another, tormented. The story is not so much a reduction to absurdity as an elevation to hyperbole of the uncomfortable side of modern life. This is not Ellison predicting the future;

it is Ellison, using a piece of SF furniture called the omnipotent computer, describing the present. Ellison's concern has shifted from earning some honest money by writing entertaining little action-adventure formula stories, to helping us see more clearly the world in which we all breathe and experience and think. This is another way in which he has grown over the years.

We could look at many other stories in which Ellison was expanding beyond the formula story. "The Beast That Shouted Love at the Heart of the World" (June 1968) certainly merits consideration. Let's content ourselves, however, with what Ellison himself said of it:

> "The Beast That Etcetera" was intended as an experiment. Consciously so. It was a serious stylistic and structural departure for me. . . . It is not a sequential story. It is written in a circular form, as though a number of events were taking place around the rim of a wheel, simultaneously. The simultaneity of events around the wheel-rim, however, occur across the artificial barriers of time, space, dimension and thought. Everything comes together, finally, in the center, at the hub of the wheel.

"A Boy and His Dog" (August 1969) also moves beyond the formula story in one crucial way (though not in many others). Like "Mouth/Scream" its settings are symbolic rather than irrelevant or predictive. In the formula story, the setting is simply the place where the events occur. It has no meaning of its own (it is irrelevant to your life and mine) or its meaning is at the level of "this may one day happen" (it predicts what our future life might be like). But the settings in "A Boy and His Dog" are reminiscent of those in H.G. Wells' *The Time Machine*: both feature two future civilizations, one above ground, one beneath; in both, these civilizations are actually the dramatizations of trends in the writer's contemporary societies rather than serious predictions; and in both, the relationship between the two societies is condemned by the writer's use of the symbol of cannibalism. Where *The Time Machine* demonstrates the necessity to share the wealth, to get the haves and the have-nots together, "A Boy and His Dog" asks us to choose between the two settings: violence above-ground and hypocrisy below. The story is slanted in favor of violence and does not suggest that any third alternative—like love, good will, or hard work—is possible or likely. The violent Vic literally consumes the hypocritical Quilla June: violence can destroy hypocrisy—and rightly so—the story suggests. In any event, in this story Ellison replaces the standard formula setting with a symbolic setting. He has discovered that it's another way to get more said in a story.

Among his hundreds of stories, Ellison has written many others which deserve the attention of readers, fellow writers and critics. I personally think of "Pretty Maggie Money-eyes," "Shattered Like a Glass Goblin," and "One Life: Furnished in Early Poverty." Others might prefer "On the Downhill Side," "At the Mouse Circus," or "The Prowler in the City at the End of the World." Nor should his recent award-winning stories "Deathbird" and "Adrift Just Off the Islets of Langerhans" be ignored. His TV scripts for shows like "The Outer Limits," "Star Trek" and "The Starlost" also form a part of his creative output.

But I want to finish my survey of Ellison's development in the structures of his stories by examining a recent production which I think offers valuable insights into Ellison the writer (and perhaps even Ellison the man). The story is "Croatoan" (May 1975). "Life Hutch" and "Blind Lightning" were neatly plotted puzzle stories set in the distant future on distant worlds. Fun and games among the stars. "Mouth/Scream" and "A Boy and His Dog" were set in futures which were symbolic of the present. "Croatoan" is set in contemporary New York. Ellison seems to be more and more concerned with facing and expressing the here and now, whether symbolically or realistically.

All writers seem to have their own peculiarities, subjects they are attracted to or subjects they never get around to using much. Ellison, for example, seems drawn to imagery of eyes and blindness. More to the point here, he doesn't write much about the out-of-doors. "Life Hutch" took place in a small building, "Blind Lightning" in a cave, "The Discarded" in a spaceship, "Repent, Harlequin" in a multi-tiered city, "Mouth/Scream" in a computer, and "A Boy and His Dog" beneath the earth and in a movie theatre and a gymnasium. Similarly, "Croatoan" is set in an apartment and a sewer, with many references to caves. Someone inclined to use Freudian criticism might want to make something of all this, but I'm more interested in the story itself than I am in the psychology of its writer.

The central character of "Croatoan" is named Gabe. His immediate problem is established in the first scene of the story. Gabe's most recent girl friend, Carol, has just had an abortion in her apartment. Gabe has flushed the baggied fetus down the toilet. Distraught, Carol orders Gabe to go into the sewer and find the fetus. It is his quest to fulfill his lady's wishes that shapes the rest of the story.

Something else has a strong influence on the shape of the rest of the story, too: the attitudes of the characters toward the lost fetus. Both Gabe and Carol consider that fetus human. Carol orders/begs, "Go after him, Gabe. Please. Please, go after him," while Gabe refurs to the fetus as "the kid" and remarks, "He was the only one who was dead." Not "it" but "he." The humanity of aborted children is assumed.

Gabe goes into the street, tries to lift off the manhole cover, cannot. He hopes that in the attempt he has done enough, but when he turns to give up, Carol

> stood silently at the curb, holding the long metal
> rod that wedged against the apartment door
> when the police lock was engaged. . . . She held

> out the rod. .... I took the heavy metal rod and
> levered up the manhole cover.

Again, critics of a Freudian bent might see some sexual implications in such a passage. After all, we have a man who can't enter a tunnel until a woman hands him a hard rod. When I asked Ellison if he were deliberately building Freudian imagery into the story, he replied, "What Freudian imagery?" The brief discussion which followed indicated clearly to me that such passages are included unconsciously in Ellison's work. They simply seem "right" to him, and their manipulation is not part of his conscious effort to shape a story.

The lid removed, Gabe enters the sewer and begins to walk in it. He passes a group of bindlestiffs huddled around a fire in an old oil drum, one of whom follows him. Gabe turns a corner and steps into a small niche to wait for the bindlestiff.

From the beginning of the story until this encounter, there are three expository flashbacks. All three give insights into Gabe's character by giving us data about his background. The first tells of Gabe's being a lawyer and of his relationships with the two women who had aborted Carol. The second continues to establish Gabe as a sexual libertine and also convinces us that, as an ex-Geology major, he enjoys being underground: "I *liked* the feel of the entire Earth over me. I was not claustrophobic, I was—in some perverse way—wonderfully free. Even soaring! Under the ground, I was soaring." This is important structurally because it helps render plausible Gabe's walking along in the sewer (instead of simply waiting by the entrance and re-emerging after a decent interval) and because it sets up the ending of the story. It makes Gabe's final decision acceptable. The third flashback traces Gabe's relationship with Carol from the time he met her till the time he goes after the fetus for her. Gabe's personality is more fully developed, as is the casualness of his sexual affairs.

This too must be emphasized: Gabe has gotten a lot of girls pregnant and has therefore been responsible for a lot of abortions. We are told this several times. The women who had aborted Carol had also been made pregnant by Gabe (and had been aborted by one another), and Gabe speaks of "their attendance at my Carols, my Andreas, my Stephanies." He wrily remarks, "I'm nothing if not potent." But the crucial thing—the reason for emphasizing this—is that, as pointed out earlier, Gabe thinks of these aborted fetuses as human, as dead children. As a result, the real issue of the story becomes the conflict within a man who has been casually creating and murdering little children and who now gradually faces up to the guilt he feels. He must find a way to save himself. The finding of that one lost fetus becomes far less important than the atoning for past sins.

I suggest that when the bindlestiff passes Gabe's niche and Gabe steps out to confront him, Gabe is actually confronting his own guilt personified. The bindlestiff expresses aloud and for all to hear what Gabe thinks of himself when he says, "You make it bad down here, Mister. . . . All of us know you make it bad, Mister." To which Gabe reacts, "He didn't want to hurt me, he just didn't want me here. Not even right for these outcasts, the lowest level to which men could sink; even here I was beneath contempt." His low opinion of himself is clear. His problem is how to raise that opinion, how to redeem himself.

The bindlestiff has no hands. Like Gabe, he is helpless.

It turns out that the sewers are infested with alligators. Ellison explains the infestation as follows:

> Frances had a five-year-old daughter. She took the little girl for a vacation to Miami Beach one year. I flew down for a few days. . . . The daughter . . . wanted a baby alligator. Cute. We brought it back on the plane in a cardboard box with air holes. Less than a month later it had

grown large enough to snap. . . . Frances flushed
it down the toilet one night after we'd made
love. The little girl was asleep in the next room.
Frances told her the alligator had run off.

I quote the passage at some length for at least two
reasons. First, it is an excellent example of Ellison's
insistence on the specific rather than the general. Many
other writers would have been content with a general
remark like "Many vacationers returning from Florida with
pet baby alligators flushed them down the toilet when they
got big enough to be dangerous, and so the sewers were
filled with alligators." Not Ellison, and his writing is the
stronger for it.

But something far more significant for the story is going
on here. An association is established among Gabe's sex life,
the flushing of aborted children down toilets, and the
flushing of growing alligators down those same toilets and
into the same sewer system. Note that the young alligators
grow up in the sewers. What about the babies?

We are not surprised when Gabe follows an alligator
deeper into the sewers. Somewhere in Gabe's unconscious,
as in ours, is that nagging parallelism: if the flushed young
alligators survive, what about the babies? Where are they?
(In another kind of story, of course, they are food for the
alligators. But not in this story.)

Gabe follows the alligator into and across a small, deep
pool. I take this to be a sort of baptism into a new life. Next
he loses that iron rod which Carol had given him and which
seemed to symbolize Gabe's casual sexuality. Then the
alligators attack him in force and he runs aimlessly,
hopelessly, terrified, at random through the sewers. When
he falls exhausted and expects death, he is discovered.

Something—an alligator?—touches him in the dark. Then
a flickering light appears in the distance. When it comes
close enough, he sees that what had touched him had been a
child with great eyes and deathly white skin, adapted to its

sunless existence. "And the light came nearer, and the light was many lights. Torches, held aloft by the children who rode the alligators."

One could, I suppose, read the ending of the story as saying that Gabe has found all the children he fathered and then flushed away, that he is no longer guilty because they are not dead after all, and that now he is going to do the right thing and assume his responsibility for their lives. However, the ending strikes me far differently. By joining the children's subterranean civilization, Gabe finds the role which redeems him for all his casual fathering and flushing. As Gabe puts it,

> Down here in this land beneath the city, live the children. They live easily and in strange ways. I am only now coming to know the incredible manner of their existence. How they eat, what they eat, how they manage to survive, and have managed for hundreds of years, these are all things I learn day by day, with wonder surmounting wonder.
>
> I am the only adult here.
> They have been waiting for me.
> They call me father.

"Croatoan" is a character-centered story. Gabe changes for the better as the result of his experiences in the story. It is a satisfying and touching conclusion to what I take to be one of the best of Ellison's stories.

Only a nit-picker would wonder what happens to the children when they grow up. "Croatoan" is about Gabe's growing beyond the joys of sex to the joys of fatherhood, an altogether different and more adult thing. It is not a story about a subterranean civilization. That exists, not for its own sake, but to help Ellison make a point about Gabe. Gabe has become a father, and of course his children are children.

And only a nit-picker would wonder about the relevance

of the "Lost Colony of Virginia" material which gives the story its title. As I hope my explication indicates, "Croatoan" is a complete and marvelous story without it. Why is it there? One suspects that the Virginia material formed the original core of the story-idea and that Ellison was reluctant to abandon it. In the context of the whole story, however, it is a minor problem.

By the way, someone once remarked—and Ellison agreed—that a major theme in his stories is the search for a father-figure. "Croatoan" reverses this theme. The quest is not for the love and security of a father but for the responsibilities of fatherhood. Gabe seeks to give love and security to others.

"Croatoan" strikes me as an advance over much of the formula and formula-like work that Ellison had written earlier because the forward movement of the story is determined by the inner nature of Gabe, rather than by any series of steps Gabe takes in order to solve an external problem. He is not a physically disabled man in a life hutch, nor is he one of a group trapped in a gigantic computer and trying to decide what to do next. He is Gabe trying to come to terms with his own guilt. The sewer may be taken as symbolic of his own evaluation of himself. This guilty man must work out his own salvation in the sewers of his own mind. The intangible psychological abstraction has been dramatized for all to see. The inner has been made outer through symbolism.

Gabe does what he does for his own psychological reasons, not because any storyline demands it. Despite his sexual success with women, he is intimidated by them: Carol intimidates him into going down into the sewer in the first place. Because he feels free underground, he walks along in the sewer unafraid and unrepelled. Because he dislikes himself and feels guilty, he agrees with the bindlestiff's assessment of him. Because the flushed alligators demonstrably grow up in the sewers, he follows one to where the flushed children live. Because of his guilt and his feeling of freedom beneath the ground, he stays with the children as their father. In "Croatoan" Ellison replaces the formula story with psychological truth—characterization, really—as the structural principle.

The central problem for the storyteller is always organization. Ellison's early stories, like "Life Hutch" and "Blind Lightning," were set in bizarre alternate worlds and were organized around a central character's solving a specific problem, usually having to do with that character's saving his own life. They were good, solid formula stories. For a long time Ellison, clearly dissatisfied with the formula, experimented with it. In "The Discarded" he killed off the viewpoint character before the story ended; in "Repent, Harlequin" and "Beast/Love" he rearranged the chronological structure of the stories so that time was no longer their organizational principle; and in "Mouth/Scream" and "A Boy and His Dog" he replaced realistic settings with settings which symbolized various aspects of his contemporary world. Now, in stories like "Croatoan," Ellison is writing stories whose structures are appropriate only to themselves and not to any preconceived pattern or reader/editor expectations. The content determines the form.

As a writer, Ellison has never stayed the same for very long. He seems to have an inherent gift for self-criticism that keeps telling him, "No, this isn't right, it's not good enough. Maybe what I ought to do is. . . ." And he'll try a new approach, a different solution to the age-old writer's problem of how to get it down on paper. (His scripts, by the way, allow him to work in another medium besides the printed page and escape its limitations that way.) Writers often get more consistent through the years; seldom do they get better. It will be interesting to see whether Ellison opts for consistency or improvement.

Where did you say that latest Ellison story appeared? I want to read it.

ELLISON
ON
ELLISON

Harlan Ellison was born May 27th, 1934, in Cleveland, Ohio. He attended grade and high school in Painesville, Ohio—a small town thirty miles east of Cleveland. His childhood, marked by unruliness and anti-Semitism (chronicled in such short stories as "Final Shtick" and "One Life, Furnished in Early Poverty"), led to his running away from home at the age of thirteen.

He promptly joined a traveling carnival touring through the Midwest, serving as "gopher," animal feeder, tent-rigger and shill for various games and sideshows. When the carnival was busted in Kansas City, Ellison was located by Pinkerton detectives who had been hired by his parents to return him to Painesville.

Though he was packed back to Painesville, and completed some necessary schooling, this was only the first of many road-running expeditions. Six months later he ran off to work as a tree-topper in a logging camp in Matawachan, Ontario, Canada. Before he was eighteen, he had worked as a tuna fisherman off the coast of Galveston, itinerant crop-picker down to New Orleans, hired gun for a wealthy neurotic, dynamite truck driver in North Carolina, short order cook, cab driver, lithographer, book salesman, floor-walker in a department store, door-to-door brush salesman, and spent ten years as an actor (off and on) with the Cleveland Play House. (In this last capacity, there are those who remember Ellison in such diversified roles as a roller-skating penguin, the victim of a psychopathic killer, and as the Christ child in an adaptation of "The Selfish Giant" by Oscar Wilde. There are those who use this last role as an argument against type-casting.)

He sold his first literary efforts in the mid-forties, while still in grade school. Two serials of five chapters each to the kiddie column of the *Cleveland News*. He was paid in tickets to Cleveland Indians baseball games. But it presaged what was to come.

At the death of his father, Louis Laverne Ellison, of a coronary thrombosis in 1949, the teen-aged Ellison moved with his mother to Cleveland, where he attended and eventually graduated from a switchblade school, East High. In 1950 he discovered science fiction, and it changed the course of his life.

He was one of the founders of the Cleveland SF Society, and began publishing their club magazine, which eventually became his personal magazine, *Science-Fantasy Bulletin* (later retitled *Dimensions*). It was through this magazine, and his fan activities in the field of science fiction that he met and became friends with most of the writers in the field, many of whom—such as Lester del Rey, Algis Budrys, H.L. Gold, Larry Shaw and Andre Norton—encouraged him to write.

He attended Ohio State University for 1½ years in 1954-55 in an attempt to further his writing abilities, but was assured he had no talent by his creative writing professor, whom Ellison suggested go fuck himself, after which time Ellison was thrown out of OSU and went to

New York to pursue his career.

Writing constantly, Ellison worked at a variety of jobs—bridge-painter, pornobook salesman on Times Square, rubbish collector in Manhattan parks—until the sale of his first few stories. His first sale was to the then-editor of *Infinity Science Fiction,* Larry Shaw. "Glowworm" (termed by author and critic James Blish as "the single worst story ever written in the field") netted him forty dollars.

Prior to this time, Ellison decided he wanted to write a novel about juvenile delinquency, and so, assuming a false name and identity, he went to live for ten weeks in the dangerous Red Hook section of Brooklyn, gathering background for his novel *Rumble* by running as a member of a kid gang called The Barons. From this basic experience came the novel, two books of short stories (*The Deadly Streets* and *The Juvies*) and his well-known autobiographical work, *Memos from Purgatory.*

During 1956 and the early part of 1957, Ellison sold over 100 short stories and articles to a wide range of magazines. He was married for the first time in 1956.

In 1957 he was drafted, and served two years with the U.S. Army. Stories of his war with the Army are legend, but it suffices to say he escaped courts-martial three times only through the intervention of Stuart Symington and then-Indiana legislator Joe L. Hensley, himself a science fiction writer and close friend of Ellison. (One of their collaborations appears in Ellison's *Partners in Wonder.*) When he was honorably discharged in 1959, he was politely but sincerely asked *not* to put in the reserve time required of all draftees. "Just leave us alone, Mr. Ellison, please?" was the sum of comments.

He was divorced in 1959 during his stint as editor of *Rogue Magazine* in Chicago. He returned to New York and re-married. He returned to Chicago to create the Regency Books line of quality paperbacks that published, among other titles, the first collection of B. Traven stories ever assembled, Robert Bloch's *Firebug,* the first nonfiction study of corruption in police departments, the first serious novel dealing with chicanery in the missile industry, Robert Sheckley's *Man in the Water,* Lester del Rey's *The Eleventh Commandment,* Philip José Farmer's *Fire and the Night* and Ellison's own underground classic, *Gentleman Junkie & Other Stories of the Hung-Up Generation* (which originally sold for 50¢ on newsstands and now brings upwards of thirty dollars in antiquarian bookshops).

It was through the purchase of a story in this book, "Daniel White for the Greater Good," and his book *Memos from Purgatory,* the former by film director James Goldstone (*Winning, The Gang That Couldn't Shoot Straight* and other films) and the latter by Alfred Hitchcock, that Ellison left Chicago and New York in 1961 for Hollywood.

Divorced again in 1962, he spent several years struggling to break into television and feature films, with only partial success. During this period (1962-63) he wrote for such television series as "Route 66," "Ripcord," "The Alfred Hitchcock Hour," "Empire," "The Untouchables" and several others.

During this time, he continued writing stories and articles and novels, ranging over a wide terrain of subjects. True confessions, westerns, detective stories, interviews, science fiction and men's magazine fiction continued to support him. However, this was a period of abject poverty.

Finally, he was given a break on "Burke's Law" and did seven scripts for that show, his work being termed "a happy cross between the mysteries of Agatha Christie and the best of Noël Coward's drawing-room comedies" by the *New York Times.*

In 1962 *Gentleman Junkie* was reviewed by the late Dorothy Parker in *Esquire* (the only paperback so honored) and extravagantly praised. It was the turning-point in his career, and the beginning of Ellison's public acceptance as an important contemporary author.

Since that time he has written such motion pictures as *The Oscar,* an adaptation of Harold Robbins' *The Dream Merchants, Khadim, Nick the Greek, Better by Far,* an adaptation of the mystery novel *Swing Low, Sweet Harriet* and others. Much of the year 1970 was spent scripting an original screenplay modestly titled *Harlan Ellison's Movie* for producer Marvin Schwarts (*The War Wagon, Hard Contract,* the Emmy award-winning *Tribes* and other films) at 20th Century-Fox. His most recent film assignment was for Playboy Productions—an adaptation of his *Playboy* short story, "Would You Do It for a Penny?", as one-fourth of the projected anthology film *Foreplay.* The film was written for Dustin Hoffman and Raquel Welch, with production and release scheduled for mid-1973.

Harlan Ellison has twice won the Writers Guild of America award for Most Outstanding Script. (1964-65 season, best Anthology Script, for "Demon with a Glass Hand" segment of "The Outer Limits"; 1966-67 season, best Dramatic-Episodic Script, for "The City on the Edge of Forever" segment of "Star Trek.")

In September of 1972 he became, unarguably, "the most honored writer in the science fiction field" as the only author ever to win four Hugos, two Nebulas and two special achievement awards of the World SF Convention.

He is one of two men to win the Hugo trophy of the World Science Fiction Convention *four times.* The other writer who has accomplished this spectacular feat is Robert A. Heinlein. Mr. Ellison has won for Best Short Story three times (1966: " 'Repent, Harlequin!' Said the Ticktockman"; 1967: "I Have No Mouth, and I Must Scream"; 1968: "The Beast That Shouted Love at the Heart of the World") and for Best Dramatic Presentation once (1967: "The City on the Edge of Forever"). His fifth award was a 1968 special citation as editor of "the most significant and controversial SF book published in 1967," a reference to the three years he spent compiling and editing *Dangerous*

Visions, an enormous quarter-of-a-million word anthology of 33 original stories by 32 writers, delineating the new directions in speculative fiction.

Of *Dangerous Visions* the leading critic in the SF field, James Blish, has written: "This book consists of *nothing but* experiments. As such, it is indeed a monument, and will be a gold mine of new techniques and influences for writers for many years to come. It may also, eventually, drastically change readers' tastes, and perhaps even the whole direction of the field." It has become the most honored SF anthology of all time.

The "Dangerous Visions" project entered its Phase Two in March of 1972 with the publication to extraordinary reviews of the second book in the trilogy, *Again, Dangerous Visions*, a massive collection of more original stories by 46 authors (including Kurt Vonnegut, Bernard Wolfe, Ray Bradbury and Ursula K. Le Guin among other top names), none of whom appeared in the first collection. Of *Again, Dangerous Visions* the Kirkus Service said ". . . it's worth its considerable weight (approx. 6 lbs.) in gilded Hugos, Nebulas, and similar cult monuments," and critic Theodore Sturgeon (in the *New York Times*) caroled, "Harlan Ellison has done it again . . . This is a prestigious book . . . It won't be put down; it won't just be ignored and go away. He has so designed it that its effect on current literature and thought will not be explosive and the father of diminishing echoes—instead, by this tactic he has turned it into a spansule, which by continuing controversy and the momentum of enlightenment . . . will go on having its effect for years . . . the book will go on provoking and infuriating and entertaining people for a long time to come."

Again, Dangerous Visions won Ellison his sixth major award in the field of science fiction, in September of 1972. At the 30th annual World Science Fiction Convention, in Los Angeles, he was awarded his second special citation— what chroniclers of the field call a "Special Hugo"—bearing the legend:

For Excellence in Anthologizing:
AGAIN, DANGEROUS VISIONS
Recognized as a Major Contribution
to the Field of Imaginative Fiction.

The sale of the Dangerous Visions trilogy (the third volume of which has not even been published, at this writing) to New American Library for $60,000 is the largest SF anthology sale ever made in the field. Its publication in trade edition has sold so well, Doubleday & Company has gone back to press for additional copies and—as the most expensive selection ever offered by the Science Fiction Book Club—in one month of availability as a SFBC selection, it sold over 36,000 copies for a gross of $180,000 . . . making it one of the bestselling titles ever produced in the field.

As a benchmark in the literature of the imaginative, the Dangerous Visions project has been called "A landmark! A Classic!" [*Science Fiction Times*]; "The single best collection of Science Fiction stories ever compiled!" [*Science Fiction Review*]; "A gigantic, exuberant and startling collection!" [*Saturday Review*].

All of this, added to the adoption of various editions of *Dangerous Visions* and *Again, Dangerous Visions* in over 200 colleges and universities as standard text for SF or futurology courses, vindicates the very special dream of new directions in the genre Ellison held when he began the massive three-volume project over seven years ago.

In late 1973 the project will be completed with the publication of the even-more-gigantic (over ¼ million words) final volume of the trilogy, *The Last Dangerous Visions.*

Harlan Ellison is also a two-time winner of the prestigious Nebula award of the Science Fiction Writers of America, having been the first recipient in the category of Best Short

Story when the award was instituted in 1965 (" 'Repent, Harlequin!' Said the Ticktockman"). His second Nebula was awarded in the category of Best Novella, 1969, for his brutal and startling story, "A Boy and His Dog."

He is currently at work scripting a film version of this story for independent production in 1973-74.

For these reasons he has been called ". . . the chief prophet of the New Wave (in science fiction) . . . a non-stop controversialist who comes on like an angry Woody Allen," by *New Yorker* magazine and "the bête noire of science fiction" by *The New York Times.* So well-known has he become that in a *Newsweek* article on science fiction (29 November 1971) reference was made to him by name alone, sans any designation or explicating adjective. His outspoken activities in the youth, civil rights and dissent movements have added not inconsiderably to the description.

In 1967 *Cosmopolitan* selected him as one of the four most eligible bachelors in Hollywood. (He was married and divorced for the last time in a ghastly 45-day imbroglio in 1965, making a total of three for those who collect statistics.)

At present he lives alone in Sherman Oaks, California, since the death of his dog, Ahbhu (who figured prominently as "Blood" in the previously-mentioned award-winning novella, "A Boy and His Dog"). He is 5'5", 137 lbs., no unusual scars, has blue eyes, brown hair, dresses in contemporary good taste, sleeps only four hours a night, has had published 25 books, over 800 magazine and newspaper stories, articles and columns, has a passion for redheads, neither drinks nor dopes, has raced sportscars, made a living singing and as a stand-up comedian, despises red cabbage, clam dips, John Wayne TV specials and people who crack their chewing gum; for 2½ years he wrote a popular weekly television column titled "The Glass Teat" for *The Los Angeles Free Press* which, as a paperback book from Ace, released in April 1970, has sold over 80,000 copies to date.

This collection of the first year's columns will be followed by a sequel, *The Other Glass Teat*. It is because of these critical writings on the subject of television that Mr. Ellison has attracted considerable attention from both the media and the mainstream. At this writing, due to "The Glass Teat" columns, a profile on Mr. Ellison is being put in work by *Time*.

He has been a film critic (*Cinema Magazine*), record reviewer and music critic (*33 Guide, Jazz Guide, FM & Fine Arts Magazine,* etc.), and a frequent lecturer, having spoken at over 300 colleges and universities including NY University, Stanford, Rice, U. of New Mexico, Tulane, U. of Michigan, UCLA, Texas A&M, Coe College, Gould Academy, University of California on many of its various campuses, Dayton Living Arts Center, San Fernando Valley State College and many others. He has been five times a Guest Instructor of creative writing at the Clarion Workshop in SF & Fantasy, and is the only Visiting Instructor to appear more than once at the famous University of Colorado Writers' Conference in the Rockies.

His writing is informed by his deep and outspokenly anti-Establishment commitment and activities in the civil rights movement and anti-Viet Nam struggles. He has been to jail as a result of actively supporting such causes as the march on Montgomery, Alabama, the Delano Grape Pickers Strike, the Peace Demonstration at Century City (where he punched a cop and wound up in the slammer), and numerous others. Having established beyond any hope of mere paranoia that his phones are tapped and Ronald Reagan has added him to the voluminous "subversive" list maintained by the state of California, Mr. Ellison sees no sense in denying that he is a militant activist, and as such has appeared on such TV talk shows as Joe Pyne, Les Crane, John Barbour, Tom Duggan, Alan Burke and others, eloquently stating that position.

His television scriptwriting credits include "Star Trek,"

"Voyage to the Bottom of the Sea," "The Chrysler Theatre," "Cimarron Strip," "The Man from U.N.C.L.E." "Outer Limits," "Batman," "The Flying Nun," "The Name of the Game," "Burke's Law," "The Alfred Hitchcock Hour" (which filmed his biography, *Memos from Purgatory*, starring James Caan), "The Rat Patrol," and "Route 66." His most recent teleplay, "The Whimper of Whipped Dogs," aired as a segment of the ABC series "The Young Lawyers," starring Zalman King, Lee J. Cobb, and Susan Strasberg.

In late 1971 and early 1972 he moved briefly (and to hear him tell it, mind-bogglingly) to the other side of the desk by working for the highest weekly fee paid to anyone on the huge Universal Studios lot in the capacity of story editor, for the ABC-TV series, "The Sixth Sense" a job he happily deserted—despite the money—after seven weeks. Cryptically, Ellison refers to working on that show as a ghastly experience akin to "reading Voltaire to a cage of baboons."

Harlan Ellison's stories and articles have been translated into sixteen languages, have been anthologized over two hundred times and included in a dozen "best" anthologies; his work has been included in high school and college level textbooks on contemporary literature and/or speculative fiction; his " 'Repent, Harlequin!' Said the Ticktockman" has become one of the half-dozen most reprinted stories in the English language (keeping heady company with Hemingway's "The Killer," Poe's "The Tell-Tale Heart" and O. Henry's "The Gift of the Magi"). Ellison's "Delusion for a Dragon-Slayer" was adapted as a Marvel comic; "I Have No Mouth and I Must Scream" has been produced as a one-act play on several college campuses; he is listed in *Contemporary Authors* (with considerable outdated and erroneous data), *Who's Who* (both the national edition and *Who's Who in the West*), *The Writers Directory 1971-73*, *Who Wrote the Movie*, *Community Leaders of America* among others, as well as *International Who's Who in Community Service* and

The Dictionary of International Biography in England.

Most recently he created (in collaboration with Larry Brody) and sold to Screen Gems and NBC, an original fantasy/occult television series, "The Dark Forces," scheduled to appear first as a one hour pre-emptive special during the 1972-73 season, to be followed by its appearance as a prime-time entry in the 1973-74 TV season.

Additionally, his SF series, "Man Without Time" (once sold to Paramount and NBC but pulled back by the creator), is currently under consideration by Universal Studios and ABC. A third series, "The Starlost," is currently under development with 20th Century-Fox and the BBC; a mini-series of eight integrated segments to be sold in England and then re-scheduled for American airing, it concerns a 200-mile-long spaceship containing humans who have forgotten Earth and who sail on an eternal trip to the far stars.

The "Ghost Story" series on NBC will feature a script written by D.C. Fontana (former story editor of "Star Trek") based on an original story, "Earth, Air, Fire and Water," written especially for the series by Mr. Ellison. It will air during the 1972-73 season.

Ellison's most recent TV script is a pilot segment for the forthcoming ABC series, "Our Man Flint." It is titled, "Flintlock," and Mr. Ellison considers it one of his best.

Quite incidentally, but as an indication of Mr. Ellison's almost pathological desire to write everything there is to write, in 1970 he moved into the field of comic book writing, having devised stories for *The Incredible Hulk, The Avengers* and *Batman.* "A Boy and His Dog" will appear as an underground comic in 1973-74, illustrated by Richard Corben.

In 1971 he wrote, co-produced and hosted a one-hour television special for educational TV dealing with SF; titled "The Special Dreamers," the highly-acclaimed and often-rerun show showcased such eminent writers as Frank

Herbert, Ray Bradbury, Norman Spinrad, Ursula K. Le Guin and Theodore Sturgeon.

In 1970 he accompanied his award-winning TV segment, "Demon with a Glass Hand," to Brazil where it was entered as a selection of the Second International Film Festival of Rio de Janeiro. It also won a special certificate of honor at the XIII International Film Festival of Fantasy at Trieste in 1970.

In 1967 he traveled with The Rolling Stones during part of their American tour, preparing a screenplay for that group that (sadly) never came to fruition, and in 1970 he went on tour with Three Dog Night, gathering material for an in-depth article that (again, sadly) never saw release due to the demise of *Show Magazine,* for whom it had been commissioned. (As of this writing, Huntington Hartford, the millionnaire ex-publisher of the magazine, still owes Mr. Ellison two thousand dollars for the work he did.)

At present, Mr. Ellison is writing for *The National Lampoon, Pageant,* functioning as SF book critic of the *Los Angeles Times,* lecturing cross-country, and writing a new series of columns for the *Los Angeles Free Press* under the general title "The Harlan Ellison Hornbook." He is completing what he calls "my most challenging stories to date" for *Deathbird Stories,* an extraordinary collection of new fictions, to be published by Scribners in early 1973.

THE
BOOK
BY
ELLISON

SCHOOL FOR APPRENTICE SORCERORS

Your assignment for tomorrow is to write a short story from an alien viewpoint. By alien we mean any viewpoint that is not human, man of today, contemporary American. This means a Martian, a troglodyte, a cat, a woman—any creature demonstrably *alien*. Got it? Then get outta here and hit those typewriters.

The next day: your assignment for tomorrow is to write a science fiction story employing the concept of labor relations. Strikes, labor practices, scabs, wages, working conditions. Future, past or present, here or Out There. Do you understand? Okay, then move it!

The next day: you have little enough to hook an editor into buying your story. Arresting title is one. Neat manuscript is another. The very best is what professionals call "the literary hook." The first line. I've been looking at your stories, troops, and your first lines are dull, flaccid, insipid, uninspiring, cliche-ridden, beside-the-point and altogether useless from a grabbing standpoint. So your assignment for tomorrow is to write me science fiction first lines that will stop a reader cold, then make him want to go on and read the stories. That's it . . . get out of here.

And the next day and the next day and the next. For six full weeks.

You think it's easy to become a science fiction writer? You think that just because SF fandom has produced Robert Silverberg and Ray Bradbury and Greg Benford and Richard Lupoff and Terry Carr and Isaac Asimov and Lee Hoffman and a host of others that *any* ding-dong can write good speculative fiction and get it published? Wrong.

Great SF writers like Chip Delany and Roger Zelazny and myself are born only once every generation. They emerge from the womb with ideas all ready to be set down on paper, and limitless craft at their fingertips. (Well, okay, I'll drop myself from that trio; it took me many years of writing to develop a style and begin to bring my work any lasting values. But the other two did it flat-out, and they are *rare*, Jim, believe me.)

But can writing be taught?

If you ain't born with it, can you ever go out and get it? Personally, I believe if you don't have that special spark from the git-go, you may be able to write good competent fiction, but you'll never become one of the memorable ones.

Okay, so we'll assume the spark is there. How do you learn to write SF with verve and dash and originality? How do you get some cornball English Lit or Creative Writing course in high school or college to give you what you need to make you a science fiction pro?

Having lectured in many Writers' Workshops all the way from the famous University of Colorado Writers Conference in the Rockies to the UCLA Seminar in SF/Fantasy, I can tell you that for the most part, 99% of the time, the courses and comp classes are worse than useless. They emasculate and stultify what budding talent a young writer may have.

And that's merely to learn how to write *anything*.

How much more difficult it is to learn to write SF!

Yet our specialized genre has one haven of learning, one genuinely authentic well of information, one extraordinary program for the aspiring SF writer: one that produces results.

The Clarion College Writers' Workshop in Science Fiction & Fantasy.

Founded in 1968 by Dr. Robin Scott Wilson of the English Department of Clarion State College—a man eminently suited for the task: consider his stories in *Orbit, F&SF, Analog,* and the forthcoming *Again, Dangerous Visions*—the Workshop had its genesis in 1967 when Wilson joined the Clarion staff. Hired specifically to establish a creative writing program at the college which would include some sort of summer program, Wilson proposed the SF Workshop and—miraculously—was given the green light by his superiors. He attended the 1967 Milford SF Writers' Conference to glean background and procedure, and to decide which SF writers he would attempt to hire as Visiting Staff. The Workshop was greeted with uniform delight by the attendees at the Milford Conference, and from the roster of writing talents available to him, Wilson selected Fritz Leiber, Judith Merril, Damon Knight and Kate Wilhelm (working in tandem), and myself for the initial season.

Returning to Clarion, Wilson began a careful process of recruiting students. Announcements were printed in several writers' magazines, in *Publishers Weekly* and the *Saturday Review.* Members of Science Fiction Writers of America and SF editors were asked to recommend potential students. The applications began coming in. Robin Wilson set up stringent qualifications to be met by applicants: they had to submit work they'd done. The obviously untalented, the fringe lunatics, the fans whose fervor for the form far outstripped their capacities for writing, the hopelessly square—these were politely turned down. The promising, the offbeat, the ferociously compelled, the vital, young or old it made no difference . . . those who could do no other than write: these were accepted.

There were twenty-four that first year. They ranged in age from 17-year-old Victor Olafson to 65-year-old David Belcher. The former a high school student, the latter a retired naval surgeon. And there was a computer programmer, and a school teacher, and a woman who wrote children's books, and a road bum and a farmboy and college students you wouldn't believe.

The course was divided up into six weeks, with Robin Wilson taking first and last weeks, hipping them to the ground rules of critical and literary and grammatical standards by which they would operate. Then the four gut-weeks were handled, in order, by Merril, Leiber, Ellison and Knight/Wilhelm. Each Visiting Instructor had his or her special way of getting into them—Fritz used kindness, warmth, wit and the power of his genius; Damon and Kate stripped each story down to its basic fiber and analyzed it syntactically, structurally, conceptually and organically, in search of wonder; I bullied, chivvied, insulted, harassed and made them write a story a day.

Classes met at nine in the morning. Frequently, the students were at half-mast. They'd been up writing all night. The sounds of typewriters coming from Becht Hall—the dorm where students and Visiting Faculty were billeted—went on into the wee hours. But they always had their product next morning. A great pot of hot coffee in the classroom, coupled with comfortable deep chairs set in a circle, usually brought them around to alertness in fifteen minutes. Or else.

Then the stories that had been submitted the day before were "workshopped." Going around the room, each student helped the author of a particular story and himself by picking the piece to pieces. Good and bad. Stylistic flaws. Character failures. Inconsistencies. Clever turns of phrase.

Original conceptions. Bad grammar. How and why a great idea was blown by muddy thinking. Said-bookism. Prolix sentences. Broken-backed phrases. Idiot plotting. Nothing escaped the eyes of students who had grown sharp and demanding during the first weeks of getting their own work flayed. And then, after the students had all said their pieces, Robin Wilson made his comments about the story, followed by the comments of the Visiting Instructor.

But as much benefit for the fledgling writers was derived from off-duty hours as in the classroom. All living together —on separate floors, policed by Clarion's own Inspector Maigret, Marie Rogers—the students and faculty spent most of their time away from the solitary typewriters on the front porch of Becht Hall ... talking, laughing, playing music, eating pizza at midnight, hustling the summer school archeology students, the "Digger" girls; getting into one another's heads, melding together into a unit dedicated to uncovering the arcane secrets of writing speculative fiction.

And the Visiting Instructors found their students so bright, so rewarding as people, that extracurricular activities suddenly became part of the Workshop: a hamburger cookout at Robin Wilson's; ghost-hunting in an abandoned church at midnight with Fritz Leiber; kite-flying with Damon Knight; Judith Merril bringing in Samuel R. Delany as a surprise lecturer; everyone going to the Clarion movie to see *The Green Slime* and destroying the audience with barbed comments; Fritz teaching fencing; going in together on the purchase of thirty dollars worth of prime steak, to be cooked in the Clarion Cafeteria and eaten before Clarion summer students (who look on the SF writers as weirdies) who are stuck with squeamy spaghetti and watery stew; playing a heavy Synanon truth game to reach into the souls and truth of each other.

Six weeks in 1968, and six weeks again this year (with Frederik Pohl replacing Judith Merril). A total of forty-three potential sorcerers. What sort of results have been obtained from this high-pressure crash-program? (Writers' Workshops are notorious for producing nothing of tangible value. If one or two out of fifty attendees at a Conference the size of Bread Loaf or the University of Colorado makes a sale, the directors crow for years. So what can we call demonstrable proof of Clarion's effectiveness?)

Well, Pat Meadows has sold several stories to *F&SF*, Grant Carrington placed one with Harry Harrison for the new *Nova* series; Dave Belcher has a brilliant novelette coming in *Orbit 5*; Lucy Seaman and Sandy Rymer landed a script assignment on "Mission: Impossible"; Neil Shapiro at *F&SF*; Evelyn Lief and Ed Bryant in *Again, Dangerous Visions* and David Gerrold's forthcoming anthology of new talents; Russell Bates sold a story idea to NBC; Phyllis MacLennan placed a juvenile novel, to be published this Fall; Diane Hollibaugh sold a short story to *Avant-Garde* magazine; Jim Sutherland hit *Again, Dangerous Visions* with a novelette; and Doubleday is currently negotiating for an anthology (with introductions by the Visiting Instructors) of Clarion Workshop fiction.

Rather startling returns on such a small investment.

Is it that Robin Wilson selected so carefully that it was inevitable his students would break through? Or is it possible that for those who love SF ferociously enough, success is guaranteed? Could it be that the Clarion Method with its integration of students and faculty is a natural for turning budding talents into selling authors? Or is there a kind of magic produced by these kids (no matter what their age) when mixed with the magics of a Leiber, a Pohl, a Knight, a Wilhelm and others? Inspired? Hell, yes. Productive? Without question. Are the runes cast correctly, is the moon in its proper phase, was a two-headed calf born, was a virgin sacrificed? Well, those Digger chicks may not be exactly virgins . . . but . . .

The Commonwealth of Pennsylvania is cutting back its educational budget. It's happening in every state. The

Establishment doesn't like the noises on campus. But one of the programs in jeopardy is the Clarion Workshop.

They'll be needing support this year. Maybe funds. Fandom has to support Clarion. Why? Because we're a tiny group, friends. We stand alone against the provincialism and retardation of our society. We dream great dreams. And teaching the sorcerers to dream the dreams properly is a holy chore. If you want to help, write Robin Wilson at the English Department of Clarion State College, Clarion, Pennsylvania 16214. Maybe . . . just maybe . . . if you've got the stuff, and you want to write SF, Robin will accept you next year. And maybe . . . just maybe . . . you can offer some solid support.

What's that? What'd you ask? What did those first lines look like? The ones that were assigned at this year's Workshop? Well, okay, if I'm going to ask you for support, the least I can do is give you a sample of the kind of wonder the apprentice sorcerers dish out. Here are a batch of first lines. You might try what *they* were instructed to try: write a solid story from any of these first lines.

1. The unemployment line was long: one vampire, two werewolves, a ghoul, three witches and a succubus.

2. Nora felt disgusted at having to eat the Catholic priest; she'd never really wanted anything to do with the Church.

3. Monroe's time machine was a real innovation: he activated it and promptly destroyed Monday, September 22nd, 1969.

4. The Indian brave, Momashay, ignored the child's protests as he swung it by its ankles and smashed its head into a tree.

5. When I am in the sun, I half close my eyes and look at my lashes. There are rainbows: that is the only beautiful thing about me.

6. His shoe swiftly consumed his foot.

7. They crucified Christ again today. I don't think he did anything this time, either.

8. Once, upon a dime, a flea ran through a quick but impressive circus act.

9. Body tense and sweating, Byron concentrated on marking off his answers; if he failed the written part of the masculinity exam, Laura would find herself another husband.

10. Sam Untermeyer was a rotten kid; even his mother said so.

11. Icarus passed overhead with sound and fire like all the wars of all time and struck the earth somewhere beyond Chicago.

12. "My son, the Polish Army, had one helluva time keeping up with combat on the semi-sweet Eastern Front."

13. He stood grinning, with a penguin under each arm, as though a man with a glass tumor was a thing of the past.

14. When Harold Plidner was four years old, he decided he wanted to be a cauliflower.

15. Sylvia took off her clothes seductively, jumped into Harry's lap and began to wag her tail.

16. One day the Pope forgot to take her Pill.

17. The road to Cinnabar was lined exclusively with the burned-out shells of school buses.

And if you think *those* show incredible imaginations at work, you should have seen the *stories* written around them. Because, you see, from June 23rd through August 1st of every year, in the drowsy heartland of Pennsylvania, there are wild and weird things happening.

There are apprentice sorcerers, gearing up for the lifetime task of mind-blowing.

En garde, Bradbury, Heinlein, van Vogt, Clarke, Herbert, Dick, Asimov, Sheckley, Zelazny, and even *you* old farts, Ellison and Spinrad.

The waves just won't stop coming, pierces notwithstanding.

GETTING STIFFED

Amateurs frequently ask, "How do I keep Them (the faceless, nameless powers the uninformed mean when they refer to editors, publishers, et al) from stealing my story-idea when I send it in?" I seldom deign to honor such questions with anything more than a cursory, "Don't worry about it." Not only because the asker's manuscript is probably on an intellectual level with that question, but chiefly because: in seventeen years as a free-lancer, I have *never* known a reputable, or even semi-reputable publisher to cop someone's plot. There are cases where it *looked* like theft or plagiarism, but when investigated it always turned out to be an extenuating circumstance compounded of lousy office procedure, righteous circumstance, inept communications with the author and a healthy dose of paranoia on the part of the one who submitted the manuscript. Again, to the last item, usually an amateur.

Oh, there are endless instances of a writer sending in a story similar to the one an editor had already bought, and thinking, when the other appeared, that the editor had ripped-off the idea and farmed it to another contributor, and I choose to think that's just rotten timing, but in all the years I've worked for, submitted to, hustled after and been rejected by magazines from the best to the worst—and pay-scale or reputation frequently did not decide which was which—I've found the men and women behind the editorial desks to be scrupulous about such matters to the point of anal retention.

Your ideas are safe. At least ninety-nine point something infinitesimal per cent of the time. I won't say it *can't* happen (this being a big and constantly-surprising universe), but the chances are so slim it ain't worth fretting over.

On the other hand, getting robbed outright is quite another matter. I don't mean just losing an idea, I mean actually having your manuscript stolen, filched, purloined, palmed, spirited away, published. And you did not receive a penny. Not a sou. Not a krupnik. Not even Blue Chip stamps. To which situation applies Ellison's First Law of Literary Brigandry:

If your manuscript was stolen and published and you didn't get paid, it was not the fault of the editor, it was solely and wholly the fault of the publisher.

Editors are good people. Some are cranky, and some are cavalier in their treatment of writers; some are inept, and some have no talent; some are out of touch with the times, and some were never in touch. But *all* of them are honest. Most of them were writers at one time or another, so they *understand.* Their reasons for leaving the honest life of the writer and entering the damned brotherhood of the blue pencil are multitudinous, but none of them are crooks.

Publishers, on the other hand, are frequently not only *schlockmeisters* of the vilest sort, upon whom used car dealers would spit, but they are equally frequently ex-manufacturers of piece goods, gadget salesmen off the Jersey Turnpike, defrocked carnival pitchmen, garment center *gonifs* whose idea of creativity is hiring a pistolero to break not just someone's tibia, but fibula as well. While this cannot be said for saints like Nelson Doubleday or Charles Scribner (he said, with just a touch of irony), there are at least half a dozen guys I would gladly name right here (were it not for the Torcon's adolescent fear of lawsuits) whose connection with The Mob, whose pokey-pocked pasts, whose absolute lack of even the vaguest scintilla of ethic or morality or business decency mark them as men unfit for human congress. They are, truly, the Kings of the Pig People. And they operate some of the biggest publishing outfits in New York.

I will, however, tell you a few fascinating stories about how I've been stiffed during those seventeen years that may provide a few moments of horrified distraction while you work out the ending of that short story for *Ellery Queen's* (a *very* reputable periodical, I hasten to add).

All in all, I've been rather lucky. Also damnably cunning and persistent, which is the key to how to avoid most of what I'm about to lay on you here. I've only been taken half a dozen times in seventeen years, with sales upward of eight hundred in magazines, and something like twenty-five in books. That isn't the worst batting average in the world, but each one of those six ripoffs stick in my craw like a boa constrictor trying to swallow the Goodyear dirigible.

The first was a short-line publisher who used to have his offices on lower Madison Avenue, in the Mosler Safe Building. Along about 1960, when I'd been released from the Army with relieved sighs (theirs *and* mine), when I was just starting to get back into free-lancing and was hurting for money, a dear friend who was working as editor on the chain of seamy periodicals with which this Jesse James of the Publishing World festooned the newsstands, called me and asked if I had a story for one of their detective magazines. The only unsold manuscript I had at the time—and there was some urgency to the request—was an absolutely dreadful piece of dreck (and I use the ethnologue specifically) about a guy who murders another guy and disposes of the body by grinding it up like a pound of ground round and flushing it down the toilet . . . all but the teeth and suchlike, which he threw in the Hudson. He gets caught when the toilet backs up. It was titled (and I trust you'll forgive me for this: I was younger and less a credit to my race in them days) "Only Death Can Stop It."

Despising myself for even submitting it, I sent it over to the editor and was mortified, chagrined and delighted when he called the next day to say he'd buy it. Thirty-six hundred words, thirty-six dollars, a penny a word. At that low ebb of financial tide, I was overjoyed to take a penny a word. Particularly for that specific thirty-six hundred words, abominably arranged in tha ghastly fashion.

I was supposed to have been paid on acceptance, but when the money didn't materialize in a few days, I called my friend the editor and made mewling sounds. He was genuinely unhappy about having to tell me the "policy" of the magazine had changed slightly: they were now paying on publication. He wasn't happy about it, but he said the Publisher was adamant on the point. I swallowed hard and said, "Wow, I really needed that money." My friend (who remains a dear friend to this day) offered to pay me out of his own pocket, but I'd heard through the Manhattan jungle telegraph that the Publisher hadn't paid *him* in several weeks, so I refused the offer. Like a jerk, I decided to wait. Men in the Publishing Industry are all gentlemen, right? Till that time, I'd never had cause to think otherwise.

Two weeks later, my friend was "let go." Sans a month's wages.

Still, I waited, feeling certain no Publisher could actually *print* something he hadn't paid for. I mean, after all, there *is* a law in such matters!

From afar, even today, come the sounds of the Muses, wailing, "Naive child, gullible waif, *moron!* "

Finally, the magazine hit the stands, and I waited very

patiently for three weeks for the check. No such creature surfaced. I began calling. The Publisher was invariably 1) out to lunch, 2) in conference, 3) out of town, 4) at a distributors' convention, 5) in the bathroom, 6) tied up with affairs of state or 7) none of the above, under the general heading "unavailable."

I talked to my friend, the ex-editor, who was also starving, who advised me sadly that we'd both (and many others) been taken, and he was truly sorry he'd hyped me in the first place. I could not find it in my heart to blame him, or conceive of redress where he was concerned.

The Publisher, however, was another matter.

So one afternoon, I put on my one and only suit, a charcoal gray item in those days, and I took the IRT down to the Thirties, from whence I sojourned forth to the Mosler Safe Building. When I reached the offices of The Great Cosmocockik Publishing Corporation, I was confronted by a cubbyhole arrangement of open-fronted offices known in the trade as a "bullpen." In each cubby a young woman sat madly blamming away at a typewriter or adding machine. It seemed to me that surely in *one* of those dingy cells some bright young lady might have been put to productive use typing up my lousy thirty-six buck check. But by then the cunning of the beast had come to the fore, and I knew such was not the case. I also knew, from the unflagging regularity with which calls from "Mr. Harlan Ellison" had been refused, that I would get no action if I used that name.

"May I help you?" asked the receptionist.

"Yes," I replied, giving her a steely, no-nonsense look. "Mr. Attila B. Hun is the Publisher here, is he not?"

"Uh . . . yessir."

"Fine. Would you please tell him that Mr. George Knowlton of the Manhattan Central Division of the Bureau of Internal Revenue would like to speak to him." It was an order, not a question. It was also a name I had made up on the spot, as is Mr. Hun's at this moment.

The young lady blanched, shoved back her caster chair and careened into Hun's lair. In a moment she was back, pressing the buzzer to release the gate that afforded me entrance, and she ushered me into the sonofabitch's office.

He started to get up, and I leaned across the desk and blathered, "I'm Ellison, you eggsucking thief, and you owe me thirty-six bucks, and if you don't lay it on me right now I'm gonna strangle you with that Sulka tie around your wattled neck!"

He started screaming for help instantly.

I panicked.

I saw a door at the side of the office, and bolted through it, just as the office help came crashing through the other door. They were all going in one direction, and I was going in the other, around into the corridor, around behind them, and past all those little cubbys . . . now-empty. In a blind stagger, but still possessed of a demonic singularity of purpose, I grabbed an enormous L.C. Smith typewriter—five thousand pounds, one of those old office standards, impossible to lift, much less carry, much lesser at a full gallop, for anyone save a madman on the verge of being apprehended and thwarted in his revenge—and I bounded down eighteen flights of fire stairs without even seeing the EXIT door through which I'd burst.

I hit Madison and ran like a kindergarten teacher who's mistakenly answered a casting call for a porno flick.

Sometime later, and many blocks further crosstown and uptown, I hocked the behemoth for seventy-eight dollars.

A clear profit of forty-two bucks.

That was the only instance of the six horror stories I have to relate in which I emerged triumphant. It was the only time I ever successfully avoided being stiffed and got paid. After a fashion.

My second contretemps with the Ravening Hordes of the Carnivorous Publishers was a transAtlantic ripoff by a German publisher who sent me how many letters God only knows, begging my permission to reprint one of my more successful stories, and imploring me to accept his offers of x number of Deutschemark for the privilege. While my German agent, Thomas Schlück, takes very good care of me indeed, this matter seemed so negligible, so unneeding of cross-communiques between my English agent, Janet Freer and me, between Janet and Tom, between Tom and the Publisher, and then back again through the lines, I decided to just take care of it myself, tell the Publisher to give Tom a commission on it, let him worry about what part of the commission he wanted to send Janet in London, and when the check arrived here I'd only have expended six months getting maybe fifteen dollars, instead of a year. Don't let that fifteen dollar business bother you. In Deutschemark it's something like DM. 12,500 or somesuch. It always looks good when it has that DM in front of it, but when you call the Bank of America and ask what's the going rate on DM today, the 12,500, (or whatever) *always* comes out to fifteen dollars.

So I wrote back and signed the contract. A year went by. I forgot the whole thing. How much time can you expend thinking about fifteen dollars? One day in the mail came a book from Germany. Nice looking hardcover. But who'd sent it, and why to me? Leafing through, I found my story, the one I'd signed to include in a nameless anthology a year before. I hadn't been paid. Several letters to the Publisher netted me a resounding silence.

Finally, I wrote Tom Schlück about it. He wrote back that the Publisher had folded his signatures and slowly skulked away into the night. Outta business. With my DM 12,500.

On the other hand, if I ever learn to read German, that book may be worth fifteen bucks. It was titled *Liebe 2002*—or, *Love 2002*: in other words, the first volume of sexy stories about the future.

I keep wondering: are they *sure* this is how Joseph

Goebbels started?

Ripoffs three and four were from "little" magazines and publications of the underground press. One was a short story solicited from an artsy-craftsy literary journal that sent me an appeal of low finances but high esteem my withered and hungry ego could not ignore. They never paid. Not even in copies, as had the ex-Waffen SS Publisher of *Liebe 2002*. The other was a series of articles I did on prognostications of ecological horror if we continue blithely raping the planet. Again, low finances were pleaded, but the Publisher got me on another of my weak points: moral obligation. I was urged to serve my world and my species. So I did the pieces, they were run, and the Publisher was last heard of living somewhere on the banks of the Delaware River, head man of a farming commune dedicated to truth, justice, ecological balance and the preservation of the area from the depredations of some kind of dam project intended to flood the valley. I cannot really find it in my heart to hate this clown, though he never paid me a cent for my work. When you deal with amateurs, you can expect to get stiffed. They just don't know any better. They have no conception of the ethical mechanics of a creator-publisher liaison. Were I to confront this dude today, and ask for what's owed me—which isn't all that much, in point of fact—he'd smile shyly, spread his hands in helplessness, and indicate the farm. "This's all I've got m'man," he'd say, and with love and truth and ecological balance he'd offer me a squash or a beet. How can you hate a child of innocence like that?

Ripoff number five is an ongoing theft, which makes it one of the more fascinating items in my catalogue of chicanery; all the more so because it's 100% legal—the Publisher has the *right* to steal from me.

Yes, I know. It confuses me, too. I'll tell you about it. And therein make a suggestion that may save you hundreds of dollars at some later date. The way it goes is like this . . .

Back in the mid-Fifties, when I arrived in New York from the wilds of the Great American Heartland, to conquer the publishing industry and carve my name in lights (or whatever it is one does on the Great White Way), I found a somewhat dismaying lack of verve at my appearance on the part of editors and Publishers. So I began writing short stories for the penny-a-word pulp markets, as had so many writers before me. It was an honorable profession in that it demanded skill and craft and reliability, not to mention the barest minimum of talent. One of the markets I found receptive to my work gave me many assignments, sometimes 10,000 words a night for week after week. I wrote many stories . . . most of which have blissfully sunk unto the swamp from whence they emerged. (When I think of those stories emerging from the swamp, I'm reminded of a comic book from the early Forties, one I adored when I was a kid. It was called *The Heap* and it concerned itself with an ex-Nazi pilot [who later became a Publisher? No, it *couldn't* be . . . well, anyhow] who crashed in a swamp and was killed, but who somehow lent his precious bodily fluids to a biological freak accident that reissued him from the quagmire as a sorta walking compost dump of sludge and yecchhh, semi-mindless and dripping ooze.)

In those days of noble struggle to make a living as a freelancer, one did not very carefully examine the check when it arrived. Usually the need for fast money was so pressing that I would deliver a story to the editor, sit there while he read it, and if he liked it take the pay voucher he would hand me and dash down to the comptroller's office to get a check drawn on the spot. It was pretty much standard practice in those days pre-Nixon, pre-Freeze, pre-Recession. Getting the check cashed before bank closing was always a dash across town, sometimes hitching a ride on the tailgate of a moving van or other Manhattan omnibus.

So it is understandable that in a rush just to get the rent paid or the typewriter out of hock, one did not look too carefully at the reverse side of the check where the Publisher had rubber-stamped in itsy type a clause of contract that said acceptance of the check meant you'd sold him all rights to the story, in perpetuity, forever, no escape clauses.

It never seemed to matter at the time.

Well, a few years ago, the Publisher, a large house with many slicks, decided to cut the last of their pulps—which had long-since gone pocket-sized—and they sold the titles and fiction backlog to what may be politely termed a *schlockmeister*. Thus, the new "publisher" was legally within his rights to reprint anything and everything paid for with one of those deadly little checks whose reverse sides bore the phrases few of us had ever even bothered to read.

Then began one of those awful nightmares writers find in their tea leaves, or whatever it is they're smoking. Old stories from ten years before, written in haste, lean on originality and fat with verbosity (at a penny a word no one in those stories ever simply *said* anything, they always *bit off the phrase harshly* [5¢], *snarled and hissed a wild string of obscenities* [8¢] or *husked the sentiments as though through a thick and suffocating fog of endless despair* [14¢]), those dreary corpses began to be exhumed. The schlockmeister dug them up, somewhichway drove a thin electric shock through them and, like amputated frogs' legs, galvanically they twitched once more into print. Adding to the utter ghastliness of the situation was the indignity of not being paid. Not required to pay, he didn't pay.

It went on that way for about a year, with story after story coming back from the tomb, and every time I'd have to explain to my friends and fans of my current work that these were, er, uh, *earlier* stories and ah, they were interesting as examples of how a great writer begins and, uh, they should take them for what they were. (Which was crap.)

Finally, after I'd won several prestigious writing awards,

the *schlockmeister* paid me the ultimate honor. He released an ALL-HARLAN ELLISON ISSUE of one of his monstrous reprint titles, and he included seven of my most worthless, inept and loathesome potboilers.

At that point I appealed to Science Fiction Writers of America, who had been boycotting the Publisher since his reprint policy had begun. Their position, and mine, was that while he was legally in the right, there was a certain sterility of morality involved in reprinting writers' work without making at least a token payment. Since it was clear nothing could stop his dredging up the *dreck,* the least he could do was pay for the privilege.

The upshot of the story is that the Publisher finally came through with payments. Twenty dollars for short stories, forty dollars for full novelettes. It was peanuts, but it opened the way to a rapprochement on the matter of reprinting bad old stories. All I had to do was write good new ones for him. For peanuts.

Blackmail is an ugly word.

And just so you gentle readers don't get the impression that only poor, shoestring Publishers are thieves, and the big reputable types are free of guilt, be advised that my most recent stiffing—years after one would assume I'd learned my lesson—has been at the hands of the world-famous Huntington Hartford, late the Publisher of *Show* Magazine.

Mr. Hartford owes me something like two thousand dollars for articles contracted-for and written to order for his magazine, but never paid for because Mr. Hartford decided to go out of business. So everything was thrown into receivership and, though he sold the magazine and apparently made a profit from the deal, he has so cleverly tied up matters with attorneys and creditors that the many freelancers who were caught in the crunch have virtually no chance of ever collecting their pay.

There is a new *Show* Magazine, but the Publisher and editors contend they aren't responsible for debts incurred by Mr. Hartford. On the other hand, Mr. Hartford's spokesmen (one never speaks to Huntington, he's off somewhere sunning at Antibes, I suppose) say everything will be settled in court sometime in 1987. Which may sit well with Mr. Hartford at Antibes, but leaves something to be desired when freelancers have to pay their rent.

For those who may have concluded from this compendium of horrors that the freelancer has only his wit and guile and tenacity to support him when faced with literary theft, it is a conclusion well-founded. There is very little a writer can do when a large publishing corporation decides to take him or her.

There are agents to help keep the losses down to a minimum, and there are writers' organizations to put on pressure, but in the final analysis the answers are to know with whom you're dealing, to make noise when the time comes and put aside fear of incurring the Publishers' wrath, and when all else fails, to become as ruthless as they are.

And no matter *what* the Famous Writer's School tells you, the life of a freelancer is *not* all roses.

There is an uncommon crop of stinkweeds in the bouquet.

The question, accordingly, presents itself: why the hell do we stay at it, instead of becoming CPAs or realtors?

The answer is so obvious, I won't bother. Just be careful.

A TIME
FOR
DARING

I've reached a point now where I don't mind people who've known me for like ten or twelve years who come up and hit me with a shot: I don't mind that at all because I know where they're at. They're consistent. But people that I've met for the first time who think they have the right, the audacity to come up and—bam! bam!—give me a real zinger, and I'm supposed to stand there and say, "ha ha, you're right, I'm an imbecile! . ." As I told Lee Hoffman, I've just about had it. I resent it and they don't really know who I am, or where I'm at, or what I do. All they know is that thirteen years ago I was a snot-nosed kid, and I'm not snot-nosed any more and they resent it. And Lee said, "They're never going to forgive you for starting where they started and going further and then rubbing their noses in it." It set me to remembering—it set me extrapolating, and to drawing some conclusions. The conclusions that I've drawn are all inextricably involved with the work that I've been doing and which I hope some of you *like*.

Many of you may remember stories that I wrote seven,

eight years ago, that I wrote for money, and wrote because, as I said elsewhere this convention, and Ted Sturgeon has said very kindly, I have to keep working. I have to keep my muscles limbered, and if that means writing garbage from time to time, okay, I'll write whatever I have to write to keep working.

But the conclusions that I've drawn, I am sure are going to offend you. And the offense is going to be greater for those of you who have known me for a long time, who've known me for years. It's certainly going to infuriate Ted White and Al Lewis, not to mention that staunch coterie who still contend that Doc Smith, God rest his wonderful soul, is the highest pinnacle of excellence any science fiction writer can attain. I knew Doc Smith and admired him vastly and would be a snot-nose again if I denigrated him. His work is something else.

So, I have to build a solid groundwork for these insults, and that requires telling a couple of stories.

Now, I suppose that generically, these are Harlan Ellison stories, because they're about me, but in a sense they're apocryphal. First a footnote:

A year or so ago, I did a television show that I liked a lot, and when I knew it was coming on I sent out some post cards to people saying, Please watch this thing. Everybody interpreted it as log rolling for a Hugo nomination. They were saying, You dirty huckster you, you swine you! Like it was terrible that I'd said, "I did a nice thing, would you like to look at it?" They all said, That's not right; you're not supposed to mention these things. So I suppose this part of my talk will be considered log rolling again for a Hugo and if so, Vote, kids. It's stiff competition.

Ten years ago the first Milford Science Fiction Writers Conference was held by Damon Knight up in Milford, Pike County, Pa., a nice idyllic spot. I wrangled myself an invitation. I think I had about eight or ten stories published, and I was living in the same building with Bob Silverberg, and writing furiously ten thousand words a night. Most of it was not really worth reading. (I had written at this point the story that James Blish called the worst single story he ever read in his life . . . He's *right!* It's awful!) I went up there, for the conference, and I had some very firm ideas about what I believed a science fiction writer should do. I had not at that point realized that I was not a science fiction writer, I was a writer, and one is not the other.

So, there I was, this little guy who had not published very much, and I was surrounded by Sturgeon and Algis Budrys, and Charlie De Vet, and Cyril Kornbluth, for God sakes, and Fred Pohl, and Damon Knight. I stood around and God, it was like being at Mount Rushmore.

And they came down on me, man, like Rutley Quantrell's army. They wiped up the floor with me. If I opened my mouth and said, "Uh," they said, "What do you mean, 'Uh'?" Everybody's a critic. " 'Uh'? What is that?" I had brought along my typewriter. I bring along my typewriter everywhere. I had it up in the room up there and I would go up and I would peck out a few paragraphs, a few lines, and they were saying, That smart-ass—what is he doing with a typewriter, trying to show us up? What is he, a wise guy?

I could do nothing right. They made me feel like two and a half pounds of dog meat.

I never went back to the Milford Conference. I couldn't hack it. It really took something out of me. I went back to New York and brooded like crazy. I didn't know if I was any good. All I knew was that I knew how to put down words on paper and people bought them. But at that time, I thought maybe that was the end. It isn't, and I learned that shortly thereafter.

Last year, I went back to Milford.

They have this Writer's Workshop and through the seven days of the conference everybody lays out a story on a big table and then everybody discusses it. But only those who've laid out a story, who put it on the line, can talk, can make a comment. No wives are allowed, no girlfriends, no chicken flickers, nothing; just the workers.

This workshop table is filled with stories, and they change them every day; they have a list of who is going to be talked about on that day. There were bits and pieces of stories that hadn't sold, short stories that were rejected maybe ten, twelve times and they couldn't figure out why, maybe a portion of a novel in work and they wanted some comment on it, things like that. Well I don't have any of those. I sell what I write, everything I write. So I went up to the Tom Quick Inn, which is where I was staying, and I sat down and wrote a short story, which I had been thinking about for some time, and I put it on this table, and the procedure is that you sit here and they go around the room from the left of you. Everybody comments once, what they thought of the story. They've all read it the night before and they lay it on you, you know; they really come on. There was a pretty sizable bunch of people there, like Keith Laumer and Norman Spinrad, and Larry Niven; Damon Knight was there and his wife, Kate Wilhelm; Tom Disch—a bunch of professionals—Sonya Dorman, who's a marvelous writer; she writes under the name of S. Dorman. (Please look for her stories; they're excellent. There is one in the new *Orbit* collection that Damon Knight published.)

I laid this story out with a couple or three carbons, so everybody could get a chance at it the night before.

Point: When I sat down to write this story, I said, I am going to write a story that is going to knock them on their ass. I'm going to write a story so good that they can't ignore it. I'm going to write a story to get even for ten years ago—that's how good that story's going to be, and it's going to be a prize winning story.

So, anyhow, they started talking about it and there's a coterie up there composed of Damon Knight, his wife Kate Wilhelm, their current fair haired boy, Tom Disch, who couldn't write his way out of a pay toilet if he had to, a few other people; they're all on one side of the room. Keith Laumer, and Norman Spinrad and Larry Niven are on the other side of the room and there's a bunch of other nice people sitting around. It started off with Damon.

Now, Damon was putting together the first *Orbit* collection, and he was looking for stories, so I said, "I'd like to submit this to you, Damon, if you like it." So he read it the night before, and it was Damon who set the tone. He said, "This is . . . I don't know what you're doing here, Harlan, I really don't. I don't understand this story, I don't know what it means, I don't know what you're going for." And I don't say anything. I'm sitting there, quiet. I'm cool.

Next, it's Kate Wilhelm. "You know I was reading this last night and I'm forced to concur with Damon's opinion. I find this story derivative and unappealing, and stupid and dumb and badly typed and everything, you know . . ." Man, I type the cleanest first draft in the *world*, baby.

So, we worked our way through the Friends of Damon Knight Society and we got around the other side of the room. Keith Laumer said, "This is one of the most brilliant stories I've ever read. It's fantastic; I love it. I think it's great." Then we hit Walter Moudy and he said, "I think it's a classic. I've never read anything quite like this. It's new, it's fresh, it's different."

One half of the room *despised* it; it was awful. Damon, needless to say, rejected it from *Orbit,* and the other side of the room loved me. So Fred Pohl was coming up for the last day, and before Damon could get to him, I hit him with this story and asked, Do you like it? He read it on the spot, and he said Yeah, I'll give you a top rate in *Galaxy* for it. I said, Thanks a lot, and he bought it. That story, "Repent Harlequin, Said the Ticktock Man," was in Fred Pohl's *Galaxy*, it was picked by Terry Carr and Don Wollheim for the *World's Best Science Fiction: 1966,* and it won the Science Fiction Writers of America Nebula, which Damon had to give me.

And as if that weren't insult, we added the injury because Doubleday is publishing the SFWA Nebula Award anthology, and it's right in there, and Damon's got to edit it and say something cool about it. And now it's up for the Hugo and it's gonna lose to Zelazny naturally, but I don't mind, because I've proved my point.

I'm going back to Milford *this* year and I'm going to give them another chance.

It seems incredible that a field as small as ours could support as handsomely and with as much room as it does, three warring coteries of writers. I'm not sure many of us are even aware of it, because we take what is given to us in science fiction magazines and since we have a limited number of editors we get pretty much what they like. But we're in the middle of a vast upheaval in the science fiction field. And I would like to try and really go into it at great length and bore the *ass* off you.

The three coteries, to begin with. First of all, there's Damon Knight's group, which I like to refer to as Damon Knight's group, and which will hereinafter be referred to as Damon Knight's group. These are the people who accept only that which they like and they have positions of a certain amount of authority—Damon's an editor at Berkley Books, and his wife Kate Wilhelm is a writer and Damon edits *Orbit*—there's this whole thing going there. They get people like Tom Disch published, and since Judy Merril is also in that in-group, she writes a laudatory review of *The Genocides* in *F&SF*. The book is not a very good book, to be nice about it, and from her review we'd have thought we had a new Nathaniel West in our midst.

Then on the other side, we've got Al Lewis's group. Now Al Lewis believes that stories of science fiction . . . I realize I'm putting words in your mouth, and you'll be able to shoot me down later, but since this is my group, baby, you'll have to sit there and put up with it. Al's feeling—and I'm sure that this is not exactly precise—his idea of the man of the future is standing on this slidewalk going through future time and he looks around and says, "look at this fantastic world that we live in, isn't it incredible, I say to you, Alice of the future 20432209, isn't this a grand world in which the buildings rise up a full screaming two hundred feet into the air, isn't this a marvelous slidewalk that's going at 25 miles an hour, and we have one over there that goes at 35 miles an hour, and another one right next to it at 45 miles an hour, to which we can leap, if we want to . . ."

Al believes that technology is the single motivating force in our culture and Al is wrong, but I'm not about to argue with him on that point. I think this field is big enough to support all kinds of dumb things. That isn't important. We sitting here are the last of the fastest guns in the west. We may find it a little difficult to understand.

For, I don't know how many years I've been kicking around, about thirteen or fourteen, something like that, but Christ, Forry Ackerman, you've been what—thirty five years in the field?

VOICE: Forty.

Forty. That's even more frightening. All right for forty years science fiction fans have been saying, *we're not Buck Rogers.* You know, like we've got some substantiality, we've got things we can teach you. We're going to the moon. "You're going where?" "We're going to the moon." I've got a copy of an article that was written in the *Cleveland News* back in '52, when I was in the Cleveland Science Fiction Society, and they sent this reporter down to laugh at us, and he came down and he did a whole nice big thing, and you know, "the room tilted at full momentum as these people decided that we were going to the moon." I mentioned to him about Heinlein's sliding roadways. You know, we could use them for conveying freight and things like that and you know he did this whole article with just this kind of tongue in cheek kind of crap that you've seen a million times after a science fiction convention or some magazine will write thinking they're very cute and clever and not realizing that they are forty years out of date.

But we've always said, *respect us,* look at us, we've got something, for Christ's sake, we're over here, you know. Ignore the western, ignore the detective story, and forget Salinger for a minute, we're over here. Right? Well, baby, I hate to shake up your nervous system, but that's been happening for about ten years. We are no longer way out there in the back eddy. The big boys are coming to us and they're looking at what we're doing. A couple of days before we came here, Theodore Sturgeon and I—we're both working doing scripts for the "Bob Hope Chrysler Theatre" —Ted had gone up there to see Gordon Hessler, one of the producers, and met Gordon and sat and talked to him for a while. I went up a couple of days later, and I walked in and Gordon came out from behind his desk. He's a lovely charming man and he said, "Hi, Harlan; I want you to meet John O'Swarz, who is from France," and this little guy, this little intense dark, electric cat leaped out of his chair and came over and grabbed my hand with both of his and pumped it like crazy and said, "Monsieur Ellison I'm overwhelmed, I do not know what to say, to meet you, to find out that you are alive, that you exist, you are . . . In one week to meet Theodore Sturgeon, and Harlan Ellison in one room is fantastic." He said, "We know your work over there, every story of yours. We know you more than Salinger, more than Hemingway, more than Steinbeck, we know you and Sturgeon." We're underground heroes over there. And it scares the crap out of you when someone comes from way over there . . . and it also annoyed me because I haven't gotten one dime from reprint money over there.

We are accepted. We're *there.* Stop pushing. (That's a good line from me. I'll have to remember that.)

The man sitting here: Digby Deal from *Los Angeles Magazine.* He's doing an article on us. He doesn't say anything, he just comes and sits, and he does. Stanley Kubrick is doing a picture with Arthur C. Clarke. He called for Arthur C. Clarke, and he said, "Look, I want to do this science fiction picture in Cinerama and I want you to do a book and I'll do the screenplay and we'll exchange bylines, me on your book and you on my movie, and we'll do a whole thing." Yeah, that's cool.

Isaac Asimov gets *Fantastic Voyage* in the *Saturday Evening Post.* He doesn't get a dime for it. That's another story. That's power politics.

The ABC Project '67 series: They go and get Robert Sheckley, and Robert Sheckley does a show for them. An hour original.

Gene Roddenberry of "Star Trek": When he started the project he had his staff compile a book of the top 1000 science fiction stories, which he sent out to all the writers who might possibly work on the series, with this admonition: "These are the best; we want *better,* we want *different.* Don't try to cop these ideas, because we know where they're at, right?" That's Roddenberry, he goes and he hires top TV writers like Adrian Spees, and John D.F. Black, who just won the Writers Guild Award, and Barry Trivers, who won it a couple of years ago. But in addition he hired Sturgeon and he had Phil Farmer working for him and he had A.E. Van Vogt writing for him, and I'm writing for him and Robert Bloch is writing for him and Jerry Sohl and Robert Sheckley ... anybody he can get hold of who knows anything at all about writing for the visual medium, who is a science fiction person. He wants to do it right. No more giant ants, or plant aphids that eat Cleveland, none of that. This is the real scan.

Every month you go in your bookstore and there are new books—in paperbacks, in hardcovers. What do you think all this is? Chopped liver? I mean, they *know* who we are. But we don't know who *they* are. We're still fighting the Civil War, friends. We're still back there screaming help, help, we're not dumb, we're not dumb. They know we're not dumb. And the more we argue about it, the more they cease to hear us, because we've now reached a noise level where no one's paying attention.

What I'm trying to say is that the mainstream has accepted us, but we haven't accepted the mainstream. We're still back here playing power politics. All us little fans are still doing our little convention thing and having our little internecine warfare and we're afraid. We're petrified to go out there and stand up and maybe get a belt in the belly.

Now this fear and terror by fandom of being assimilated is like the same thing that every ethnic group has in its ghetto, like "you're gonna marry him, he's a goy what is that?" Right? Or "I don't wanna see our race mongrelized." That's exactly what it is. We're afraid to get into the big stream. Somebody like a Herman Wouk will come along and do *The Lomokome Papers*—you all remember that garbage —and we'll say Well, see: that's what's going to happen to us. But we ignore *Cat's Cradle* and we ignore *White Lotus* and we ignore *Clockwork Orange* and we ignore *Only Lovers Left Alive* and all of these pure science fiction books, which are done by people outside the field, who have taken the ideas that we've put forth, who have used all of these tremendous concepts that we spent thirty-five years developing and they're using them; it's a matter of course for them. They say, "Sure these guys have proved it already; we don't have to. We can go ahead from there."

Now, what I'm trying to say is that we've become important to the mainstream. Truly important. This is steam engine time for science fiction. *It's science fiction time.* Science is passing us by. We're on the moon and we're doing the freezing the bodies thing, and "Time Tunnel" comes on TV this Fall (it's a piece of crap, but it comes on, and people will know what it's all about, going back in time; they'll be able to understand that). So it's our time now, friends.

Now is when we catch the gravy.

Now is when everything pays off for us.

Now is when a man like Sturgeon is going to collect what he's been due for all these many years. You know: like writing penny a word and two-cent a word stories for the pulps; now all of a sudden he's going to get three, four, five, six, $10,000 for a television script, for a book. This is what we deserve. We paid our dues . . . it's time for us now.

But we're being held back . . . we're being fettered in many respects and torn apart by the conservatives. Now, no offense. We're being hamstrung in the magazines and in the books and by the entrenched power structures—you know, the Damon Knight gang—and by the people among us who are short-sighted, who continue to contend that they are the far seekers, that they are the future-seers. They're the ones that still want the stories that were written 25 years ago, for Christ's sake. And every time somebody tries to do something new, they say, "Whew, where is this cat at . . . what is he doing?" It's like in the jazz idiom: a man like Ornet Coleman, five to eight years ago started blowing new sounds and a few people picked up on it and said, "this guy has got it . . . this man is saying something." And everybody else said, "Huh?" They're scared 'cause they don't know where it's at and they're afraid. They're afraid they're going to get left out in the cold. They're afraid they're not going au courant. They're not going to be with it, and so they put it down. And that's what is happening to an awful lot of important science fiction.

A man like David Bunch has been writing for ten years. The only place he could get his stuff published until recently was in Ron Smith's *Inside Magazine*—you know, a fanzine—or a few other places, literary magazines, little places, where he could sneak it in and they didn't know it was science fiction. He would say that this was a parable of the future. *Now* Bunch is published in most of the bigger magazines, and his work is understood and seen because we have caught up with *him*. You know, we thought *Demolished Man* was a big step forward . . . that was a nice story with a lot of interesting typography. The guys who were really writing it—the guys who were really saying it—are the guys we have *shamefully* ignored for years.

It's a time for daring. Now is the time for brilliance and invention. And no one is suggesting that the roots of science fiction be ignored or forgotten or cast aside. Solid plotting, extrapolation, trends and cultures, technology—all of these things are staples that are necessary to keep the genre electric and alive because that's what we are. That's what makes us not *Peyton Place*. Okay: granted. But why should we who know and love this medium see it expand its frontiers in the hands of William Burroughs and John Hersey and Anthony Burgess and Thomas Pinchot while we stare back in wide-eyed wonder, because we never considered writing *A Clockwork Orange* or *White Lotus* or *The Crying of Lot 49* or *Nova Express*?

Take a look at Burroughs' *Nova Express,* friends. Now, that's science fiction and it's fresh and it's daring and it's different. And it will beat out any bloody thing that James Blish or Damon Knight have written in the last five years.

Now I don't mean to pick on any single person expressly. There are dozens of writers I could point to. Writers whom you respect and if they were standing up here you would come up and say, "Can I have your autograph?" And you should, because they paid their dues. Mr. Van Vogt was here and I don't know if he still is here—I would hate to pin him when he isn't here—but Van Vogt's stuff, in many ways was very daring . . . twenty-five years ago. But his stuff isn't there any more. There are new guys who are doing it.

Why should we have to stand back and wince in pain as the Herman Wouks, the Ayn Rands, the Rosser Reeds demean our literary form? Why should we have to sit there and say, "These guys are doing it because we didn't have the guts to do it"? And have to put up with their bad writing?

We're lucky we've gained a few good writers—writers like Burgess. But we've got an awful lot of schleps, too. And it's a pain that we have to sit here and put up with it.

The tragedy of what we are *now* is the tragedy of what we've been doing for thirty years. We've been leaching the vitality out of our best writers—our Sturgeon, our Farmer, our Philip Dick, our Kurt Vonnegut. We've sent them off to other fields because they couldn't make a living with us. They had to write for the "in-group." They had to write for us and please us and pleasure us because God-forbid they should come to a convention and have someone say, "What do you mean—what is *Inside-Outside* actually about, Mr. Farmer—what are you trying to say? What are you doing? Ha?" We've sent them off to the other field. Vonnegut to the mainstream comedy novel; Sturgeon to Westerns, movie adaptations, TV writing; Farmer to white-collar jobs, too many paperback commitments; Phil Dick to the edge of lunacy. This is what we've done to our good writers, because we've been too busy reading the hacks. And why have we been reading the hacks? Because we can understand them; they will give us a nice technological thing that we can play with and toy with and masturbate with and we like that a lot. But when they really demand something of us, when they write something really new and fresh and different and inventive, we don't know where they are. We look at them and we say, "You missed that time, but you'll make it the next time; maybe you'll write *Slan* next time, baby," We complain that our best men have left us. That they have gone on. That they deserted the ship. And it's precisely the opposite: the ship has deserted them. They have outgrown us. They've gone away because they're bigger than us; they need more, they have to have more. And they find it selling mainstream stories which you laugh at; you say, "Well, you know, if I want to read that crap, I'll read the mainstream." I'm not talking about book-of-the-month-club selections, friends; I'm talking about stories that demand inventiveness and demand a bigness, a fullness from the writer that you can't get most of the time out of science fiction.

Because we have literally bound ourselves into a bag that we can't get out of.

For too long we have allowed those of us who formed our idiom to tell us what is good and what is bad. We've allowed them to say, "Well this is a good story, because it's in *Analog* and this has gotta be a bad story because it's in *Amazing*. Well, now if it's in *Amazing,* probably it's because they're reprinting . . ."

These writers have grown too big and too important and too dedicated to their art and that's the operable phrase. Before they are science fiction writers, they are *writers,* and you can read them in any other idiom, any other genre, and they will be just as sharp; they don't demean themselves. Somebody said yesterday, "He was lost in Hollywood writing for television." Well, I got so lost last year, friends, writing science fiction for television that I won the top award of the Screen Writers Guild. I beat out a Purex Special, a Chrysler Theatre, and the pilot for "Run for Your Life"—on a show that had a budget like $1.98. And it was pure science fiction—it wasn't anything else.

You don't get lost if you're a writer—if you really work. These people have left us for the very simple reason that they're too big and too talented to be constrained by our often vicious, often ungrateful little backwater eddy. They burst into the mainstream and the mainstream has taken notice of them. Sturgeon comes to Hollywood and Hollywood knows it. His name is in the trade papers, and the producers want to see him. Alan Arbor used to be the producer on "The Fugitive"; he's now doing the new one, "The Invaders." He calls for Sturgeon. Gene Roddenberry wired ahead to New York—"Have Sturgeon there; I must talk to him. I want him to work for me." You walk on the set and actors who don't know much of anything except what their own faces look like, say "Theodore Sturgeon?" And they know him. This man isn't unknown; no one who is *good* is unknown. And yet at the same time, here we sit and you have the audacity to make me a "Guest of Honor" and I'm nothing—and Vonnegut has *never* been a Guest of Honor; he's never been *asked* to be a Guest of Honor. Here's a man that has written a novel that has been one of the seminal influences in our field. Something that almost any writer can look at and say, "Yeah, it's so simple to write like that—that you can't do it." Great art looks simple, but it isn't. It's like watching Fred Astaire dance—try it and you'll fall on your ass. Vonnegut is big—he's important—and we gave the Hugo to Clifford Simak for a novel that any one of us who write science fiction could have written.

It's a crime.

It's a shame.

And we've been doing it for too long. I stand before you as nothing more, really, than an emissary of the open mind. If you're going to continue to call yourselves science fiction fans—the chosen people—we see the future—the golden ones—all of that crap we've been swilling down for twenty-five, thirty years, you damn well better be able to see what's in your midst. Because you are losing men that you should have working for you. You are losing men that you are ignoring and laughing at and you're losing men who are going to change your form and put it where it's supposed to be: on a level with all great art.

A VOICE FROM THE STYX

It is possible this reviewer is one of the very few devotees of speculative fiction who has not as yet devoured (or allowed himself to be devoured by) Frank Herbert's *Dune*.

I have attempted to read the book several times, and one day I shall overcome the lethargy that assails me each time I undertake the chore, and get it read. Until recently, my inability to read Herbert filled a corner of my critical mind with guilt. One knows there are things one *should* read, if one is to understand the genre fully, if one is to be able to speak with lucidity and a sense of history on the problems and trends current in the form. One knows one *should* read van Vogt's *World of Null-A*, Doc Smith's Lensman series, Huxley's *Brave New World*, J.T. McIntosh's *One in Three Hundred* or Poul Anderson's first van Rijn novel, *War of the Wing-Men*.

But the reader coming to these books already having been convinced they are "important" is opening himself wide to a paralyzing shock of realization. These are not only *un*important books, they are—frequently—badly-written books, ineptly conceived books, characterless books, little more than polemics or problem postulations and—most unforgivable of all—they are dull and boring books.

My fear of finding this to be true of *Dune* may be what it is that keeps me from wading through "the first 30,000 dull words to get to the really great stuff beyond" of which others have apprised me. I hope all of this sensed tragedy is groundless. I want very much to enjoy a book so many people have assured me is "important." But oddly enough this is a repetition of an experience that occurred once before with a Herbert book; tagged "important" by all who read it, I was unable to get past the first few pages of the first installment when it ran in *Astounding Science Fiction* as "Under Pressure" in 1955-56.

I speak, of course, of the fully novelized version of that "classic" novel of men under stress in a confined artificial universe under the ocean, *The Dragon in the Sea.* Now, twelve years after its initial appearance, I have applied enormous gobbets of stick-to-it-iveness and have read Frank Herbert's "important" book of 1955-56.

Reluctantly, my instincts of over a decade ago have been proved well-grounded.

It is seldom a readable book; it is never a good book; it is frequently an appalling book.

The critic coming twelve years late to his subject risks (possibly deserved) obloquy from not only the author, but from readers and fellow critics. He has all the benefit of hindsight and none of the responsibility of adventurous opinions. He can be cited for heating yesterday's hash, he can be reviled for attacking a hallowed institution, he can be discounted as merely trying to establish a reputation for critical analysis on the merits of his betters whom he seeks to attack for personal gain. Knowing this is front, I still feel compelled to dwell briefly on *The Dragon in the Sea;* to open a closed file, a dossier stamped FINALIZED, in an effort to isolate a literary embolism that even today causes discomfort in the bloodstream of speculative fiction.

(And in all fairness, aside from my admiration for Herbert the Man, my carp is more with John W. Campbell than with Herbert the Writer. And since the editor is the more influential of the two, it is *his* millstoneage upon which I will center the force (such as it is) of my arguments, thereby preserving my friendship with Herbert.)

The Dragon in the Sea, it seems to me, is a painfully precise example of the immolation which results when Campbellian technocracy writing is allowed to carry itself to its final extrapolation of style and content.

To refresh the memories of those who encountered the plot some time ago, simply put it is the story of a four-man crew of submariners in the not-too distant future, on a mission to the oil fields of the Enemy Power, to effect the pilferage of enough tonnage of vitally-needed oil to fill the mile-long "slug" their subtug tows. There is a spy on board. There has been frequent "shattering" of subtug commanders. A psych man trained as an electronics officer is put on board the subtug *Fenian Ram* by Security with the dual mission of locating the spy and finding out how it is the Enemy Powers are able to blow up so many subtugs with such methodical precision . . . and to telemeter the psyche of the *Ram*'s commander, Sparrow.

"Long John" Ramsey, the electronics/security/head thumper encounters 1) the totally-unexplained murder of a Security inspector, 2) the sabotage of the atomic pile, 3) the hostility of the crew, 4) the suspicion that he himself is the spy, 5) rampant religious fanaticism on the part of Sparrow, 6) the presence of an Enemy beaming system on board, 7) the breaking-loose of the manual control damping arm in the pile room, threatening to dump the atomic pile on its side, 8) loss of ballast in the slug, 9) constant pursuit by EP subs, 10) assorted paranoia and psychosis and 11) everything else.

Despite all of this, there is substantially nothing happening in this book. Four men in an enclosed space should be expected to interact in a highly emotional and dramatic manner. The nitwittery that occurs down below in the *Ram* is about as dramatic as Jack and Jill's ascent to fetch the pail of water. Everything is happening inside them, and if any of it manages to get out, it is most actively demonstrated by the instance of First Officer Bennett's beating the crap out of Ramsey for some reason not sufficiently explicated by Herbert to make it matter much.

The menace of the EP is a peripheral one, no more omnipresent in the reader's mind than it is on the warning board of the *Ram,* where it appears as a signal. A signal, mind you, to which the crew reacts about as forcefully as they might to a splinter in the finger.

Well, then, if there is no menace, if there is no plot, if the interaction of the characters is shallow, then why am I, and why are you, and why is Herbert here? Is it for the richness of characterization? Hardly. Bennett is Garcia is Sparrow is Ramsey. One and all each is the same one. They are faceless, interchangeable, all sound alike, all act alike, think alike. Artificial identities are attempted, stuck on like putty noses. Garcia (!) speaks with a British accent. Which he loses on a moment's unnotice. And when he has it, it is Herbert's conception of British mannerisms—'bloody heroes,' etc— and is not in any observable way different from the homogenous manner of the other three men.

Ah. I see. So it isn't the depth of character. Well, then, is it some incredibly perceptive insight into the human condition? Some analysis of men under stress, under pressure? If it is, then Herbert has failed dismally; he makes the standard point that war cripples victor and vanquished alike, that war is hell, that war is interminable, and that men need brass bands playing when they go out to make war so they will want to come home again. All of this is cotton candied with some highly specious parlor psychiatry, most of which (though highly dubious) is obvious to the most slack-jawed reader from the outset, yet which is sprung in bits and pieces throughout the book as genuinely eye-opening. On the contrary, it is yawn-provoking.

The simple fact is, the sole reason for the existence of this novel is the gleeful and meticulous explication of the minutiae of hardware aboard the *Fenian Ram*. This is a gear-and-grommet story. It is an engineer's daydream. It is a chromium gearshift. It is a stainless steel thundermug. It is a guided tour down the gullet of The Machine God. It is not a novel, nor a study of people, nor an attempt to point a moral, or tell a story, or entertain a reader; it is shop talk. It is screwdriver and spanner bull sessions among men who think in micro-fractions. It is anti-story.

And it is bad, as a result.

In any definition of speculative fiction, there is an unspoken corollary: the most effective fiction in the genre is that which touches on reality in as many places as possible while maintaining the mood of speculation. I would have used "sense of wonder" rather than "mood of speculation," had the former not fallen into disrepute through misuse. What I am saying, in effect, is that a kind of magic realism must be established in the story if it is to be an expert example of the best the field can produce. It is a balance, a symbiosis perhaps. The reader must be able to draw the lines of extrapolation from his own experience or environment—the world in which he lives today—through the intervening linkages of logic, emerging at the new place to which the writer has taken him.

When these touchplaces with reality fail to appear, the story suffers. Proportionately, the fewer touchplaces, the weaker the story in terms of the readiness of a reader to adapt his thinking to meld with that of the writer.

Herbert's *Dragon in the Sea* contains touchplaces of only the most casual sort: submarines, war, men under stress, primary emotions. These are insufficient to weld the story to "the real world" and as a result, the boredom mounts in direct relation.

One simply cannot *care* what happens to the stick-men who populate this novel. One cannot believe their war, cannot value their cause, cannot tense at their danger, in fact can involve oneself as a reader in only the most casual way.

It is this lack of the necessity for involvement on the part of a reader that typifies a kind of writing John Campbell has championed in *Analog* (under its various logos and titles). What began as a New Wave in the Forties with Campbell's rejection of the Crustacean Period in speculative fiction, what sailed along smoothly as practiced by Kuttner and Heinlein and Sturgeon and even L. Ron Hubbard, has come far past the end of its passage, and now represents something like a return to the T. O'Connor Sloane image of what a *good* science fiction story should be.

Now you will notice that for the first time in this discussion, I have used the term science fiction, rather than speculative fiction. There was calculation in so doing. *Dragon in the Sea* is *science* fiction, and not *speculative* fiction, and therein, I contend, lies the nubbin of the problem. For by adherence to the syllogistic logic of Campbellesque *science* fiction, most of the values of good storytelling necessary to the construction of valid *speculative* fiction have been lost . . . or worse, ignored.

The time for science fiction is past. There is more than a self-conscious re-identification in the daily more-frequent use of the phrase speculative fiction. It is a seeking toward more precise definitions. It is quite all right, among ourselves in the SF fraternity, to point to something and say, "That's science fiction," but for the mainstream which we are rapidly absorbing, the confusion has lain precisely there. We point to *Cat's Cradle* and we point to *The Child Buyer* and we point to *War with the Newts* and we point to a thousand other items, no two even remotely alike, and we are dismayed when the *New York Times Book Review*

Section tells us: *A Canticle for Leibowitz* can't be science fiction, because it's good.

To the eradication of this confusion, I would suffer infinitely greater insults than those leveled by critics who feel the substitution of "speculative fiction" for "science fiction" is a conscious attempt at ostentation.

It seems to me that novels such as *Dragon in the Sea,* ponderous with the weight of its own science, sluggish with the accumulated gimcrackery of engineering persiflage, foundering under the burden of hardware that can never substitute for story, is one of the reasons why we are today struggling toward a new definition—and a "new thing," if I may be permitted—of the form.

The Campbell heavy-science story as typified by *Dragon in the Sea* is a sterile art-form to pursue. It is the ultimate descendant of all the things-wrong in the work of van Vogt and George O. Smith and Lee Correy and Hal Clement. It is the usurpation of character and plot to the ends of the engineer. The further into his own encystment John Campbell has grown, the more immolated have become the novels he publishes. The progression is fascinating to watch in terms of the writers he influences. Hal Clement has progressed from *Needle* and its highly evocative characters to *Close to Critical* which is barely readable. And the important observation is that Clement seldom writes *for* Campbell these days. The influence goes far beyond the pages of *Analog* the editor controls. In some ways it is even *more* fascinating to list the important writers of today who have *never* appeared in *Analog,* nor would they find a welcome there: Philip Jose Farmer, Samuel R. Delany, Roger Zelazny, Avram Davidson, Piers Anthony, to name only a few of the more obvious. Or the writers who have not for a long while written toward Campbell at all: John Brunner, Sturgeon, Knight, Blish, Leiber, del Rey—all of whom at one time or another worked in the Campbell idiom.

More and more, Campbell has leaned toward writers who are not writers; engineers and scientists who have been able to transpose theories and mechanical developments in their certain fields into shallow stories, mere vehicles for the science. It is this exodus of the real writers and the insurge of amateurs that has made *Analog* for the most part unreadable, and removed it yearly from the Hugo competition for Best Magazine. (I submit this is the most telling argument of all that Campbell has passed his time of importance in the field. The fans who vote for the Hugos are easily swayed; their choices are made usually on the basis of trend and loudest word-of-mouth publicity. When an overall trend in the field is felt, it shows up in the broader categories, such as Best Magazine. And *Analog* has not even been in the running for half a dozen years. This, for the magazine which allegedly sells the most copies in America, seems highly unusual, until one considers that those copies are being sold to the other members of the bull session—other engineers and scientists.)

Campbell's disenchantment with the fiction is obvious. *Has* been obvious for ten years and more. His enthusiasms have ranged through Dianetics to Scientology to the psi theories of the Hieronymous Machine and out the other side into pure engineering concepts. Consider the current issue of *Analog* with its cover and major emphasis on a non-fiction article. And then consider the authors of the stories. With the exception of Anne McCaffrey, who is a writer and not a scientist, the table of contents contains one writer who is employed by AVCO and makes his primary living in science, one pair of writers who win that appellation by the barest minimum standards of craft, and two names who are as much non-entities as the stories they proffer. The first forty-four pages of the issue are pure science fact, and much of the rest of the magazine is the same, thinly disguised as science fiction. For whom are the *speculative fiction* writers working? Certainly not Campbell.

If one wishes to read Clarke, one must go to *Playboy*. If one wishes to find Sturgeon, one must turn on television. If one wishes to encounter Sheckley or de Camp or Asimov one must buy their books. Campbell has been compelled to turn to the untalented amateurs, for the most part, not because he has been deserted by his writers, but because *he* has deserted *them*. When his interest in the fiction fell off, his receptivity to the men who could produce it vanished.

A pause to let the mind boggle: can anyone conceive of Campbell publishing an issue of "the new thing"?

I'll wait for you to come back.

Long enough?

Okay, let's resume.

Campbell, as champion of hard science, has created an aura about *Analog* that makes even the *submission* of non-Campbellesque hard science stories unthinkable. (How often have I heard a writer deny he is a "Campbell writer" merely because he has sold him three or four stories; how often have I heard a writer joke he was going to send a certain story to Campbell because it was precisely the kind John did *not* buy; and how often has John bought stories highly atypical, thereby seemingly dispelling the theory that he is a one-track editor. The last, of course, is a case of a minor lapse in the main drive of Campbell's interest, or the supreme compliment that a non-Campbell story was so well done he was forced to look out beyond his nose to remember his past greatness as a selector of memorable fiction.)

This aura has produced novels of the *Dragon in the Sea* variety. Clanking, clattering, caliginous catastrophes containing can openers, cliches and case studies not characters.

Too often when laymen or non-readers decry speculative fiction, saying, "I can't read that stuff," what they refer to is the Campbell dull-science novel. Without realizing it Campbell has come full circle, and has metamorphosed into T. O'Connor Sloane.

Unfortunately, he has dragged along with him some very good writers. Frank Herbert—at least twelve years ago—was one of them. Those who are reading Herbert now can make their own final analyses.

To all intents and purposes, Campbell has removed *Analog* from the field, it is inaccessible to the bulk of writers currently practicing in the genre. And it is beyond the interest range of much of the audience it once reached.

Or rather, let me say, it still interests readers of science fiction. But what of the growing horde of seekers after that new sense of wonder called speculative fiction?

We come now to the inevitable fractioning of the form. What is "mainstream fiction"? It is Guthrie's *The Way West* and *The Big Sky*. Which are westerns. It is *Miss Lonelyhearts* and *The Day of the Locust* by Nathanael West. Which are religious allegories in contemporary settings. It is John D. MacDonald's novels of Travis McGee. Which are adventure/suspense novels. It is Myrer's *Once an Eagle*. Which is a war novel. It is Baldwin's *Another Country*. Which is a love story. The main stream, as nobler critics than myself have long noted, is composed of many smaller tributaries. The genre novel—in reality—no longer exists, save when it is so hopelessly inbred (as with the most inept cowboy novels or slanted "nurse" and "gothic" novels) that it aspires to no greater stature in the pantheon of Art.

Only in speculative fiction do we still seem to retain the semblance of doing-our-thing with no (or little) recognition of what goes on in the larger arena. I think the operable word in that previous sentence is *semblance,* for in point of fact the novel of speculative fiction has undergone so many changes and directions in the past ten years that today, as I write this, August 1st, 1968, *Publishers Weekly* (v.194, n.5) reviews John Brunner's forthcoming Doubleday SF novel *Stand on Zanzibar* not in the science fiction section, but as a mainstream fiction offering, side-by-column with *The Best*

American Short Stories 1968, John Barth's *Lost in the Funhouse* and Hermann Hesse's *Beneath the Wheel.* The reviewer makes no bones that the book is SF, but says of it:

"Doubleday classifies the whole thing as science fiction, but it's far from the conventional science fiction-fantasy category of writing."

The reviewer also said, after praising the book inordinately, and directly leading the reader to understand that this is a book of rather heroic proportions, "Anyone who doesn't want to work pretty hard for his cautionary tales might take (preceding comments on the book's intricacy) as a hint."

This review, and more what it implies than what it openly says, should give us pause for consideration of the current state of the SF novel in relation to the mainstream. There is a definite attempt here to single out *this* book as something above and beyond the "conventional SF-fantasy category of writing," whatever the reviewer may think that is. Is this merely another attempt to label a *good* book as something apart from speculative fiction, as though Hersey's *The Child Buyer* or Levin's *Rosemary's Baby* are *not* SF-fantasy merely because they *are* good?

I think not. The tone of this review is much too informed, much too on-target. I think what the reviewer is subliminally saying is that much of the speculative writing being done today *is* genre: in intent and in execution. And that Brunner's new one far excels that mingy labor.

For it now becomes clear that the fractioning of the genre has for ten years been in progress. We now have war novels of SF (*Bill, The Galactic Hero; Starship Troopers*), we have westerns of SF (*War of the Wing-Men; The Horse Barbarians*), we have religious allegories (*Thorns; Lord of Light*), and we have love stories, historicals, novels of manners. These last three types bring me through a somewhat underground route to my topic of discussion, Anne McCaffrey's new Ballantine novel, *Dragonflight*—an historical love novel of manners.

This reviewer confesses in front that he comes to the subject of women writers with something approaching paranoid ambivalence, leaning slightly more toward antipathy than delight. Until fairly recently I was firmly convinced that writers who were women amounted to very little. I cast back historically to find precedent to make me reverse my decision, and the best I encountered were the Brontes, who, at best, wrote elegant soap operas. But within the past five or six years I fortuitously mortared up the gaps in my literary education with the likes of Isak Dinesen, Flannery O'Connor, Shirley Jackson, Dorothy M. Johnson, Zoe Oldenbourg, Mary McCarthy, Charity Blackstock, Barbara Tuchman and the incomparable Dorothy Parker (whom I'd always adored, yet somehow managed to exclude from my theory by a feat of unmatched speciousness). I had managed, also, to exclude Leigh Brackett, Andre Norton and Catherine Moore. Obviously they weren't "women writers." They wrote like men.

It may seem an oversimplification, not to mention a crotchet, but men write like men (most of the time) and women write like women. There is a gentleness, a softness, a frustrating lack of tensile strength in the writing of most women. Best typified by the works of Fanny Hurst, Frances Parkinson Keyes and Agnes Sligh Turnbull. We won't even mention Edna Ferber. My theory—that now-hoar-encrusted theory—was that women, having been reared with a Jessamyn West "friendly persuasion" way of thinking, were incapable of truly coming to grips with those flash-points of conflict that invariably result in emotional, gut-level reformations of character, not to mention naked violence. Try to think of a woman having written the scene in *Billy Budd* where Billy, chivvied by the detestable Claggart, incapable of vocally defending himself, kills the Mate with one blow.

Morris Renek, in "Reflections on Violence as a Literary Tool" (*Story Magazine*, May 1967) puts it thus: "In

Herman Melville's *Billy Budd,* for example, the act of violence clearly takes the place of speech. Billy's blow articulates his anguish against tyranny where his tongue cannot. Violence has this illiterate coherence. Everyone understands a sock on the jaw; when language fails, there is the fist."

Written by a woman? Unthinkable.

Or try to conceive of a woman having written Faulkner's *Intruder in the Dust,* or a woman's view of the scene in *Tropic of Cancer* in which Henry Miller describes fucking the Jewess under the stairs, all the while surreptitiously ransacking her spilled purse for subway fare. Or a woman understanding the gauze-like theory of Those Who Are Doomed By The Universe that eternally separates Henchard from Farfrae in Hardy's *The Mayor of Casterbridge.* These are points of view, last extremes of the human condition that women seem apparently unable to manipulate.

As my secretary recently said (in jest, but with more insight than she had thought), "Are women writers like women drivers: licensed, but not really in control?"

Well, I think that may be a bit strong. As I've noted, there have been women—no, make that *female*—writers who could show most *male* writers which end of the pencil was the business end. Comparisons between Katherine Anne Porter and Leon Uris instantly become invidious. But still there remains the stigma attached to a work of fiction by a woman; and in SF the stigma is at its most apparent. One need count no further than one's fingers to total the female writers who have made it in this specialized category.

Whether the explanation for this be inherent in the state of social subjugation into which women have historically been forced, only now breaking down and becoming sufficiently memory-dim to allow women a flexing of their literary muscles, or because there is an inescapable truth in the theory that women are too home & hearth-bred to provide them with the raw material of creativity that intense Art demands ... I cannot say. Each school has its proponents. At this point, and in part due to Miss McCaffrey's recent writings, I find myself having deserted the latter theory, and inclining more toward the former.

Yet—and again because of McCaffrey—I do not swallow the "woman in bondage" philosophy whole. For here, and now, in this enlightened era, we have a novel by a woman that tackles some hard SF topics, and if it fails in parts, it is those parts to which the female orientation has been brought, and applied.

As aside, though quite in line with the above: how would this book have read (I cannot keep myself from wondering) had it been written by Theodore Sturgeon, with his incomparable understanding of all the manifestations of love? How would it have read had it been done by Keith Laumer, for my money the very best straight action writer we have these days? How would it have read at the hands of the Kuttner-Moore team, with his sure sense of the ironies of social protocol and her deep pool of feminine wisdom expressed in terms a man could relate to? And what would it have looked like, on the other hand, had it been subjected to the penchant for ecological minutiae of a Hal Clement? How would Mack Reynolds or Harry Harrison have burlesqued it? This is the kind of novel that suggests so many variable ways of having been told, that one inevitably wonders what its shape and structure would have been had it been done better or worse by any one of a dozen different craftsmen.

But obviously, and sensibly, since we have here a version written by Anne McCaffrey, that is the one with which we must deal. And for the purposes of explicating the fractionalizing of the genre ... for the purposes of examining the expertise of female writers with the tools and modes of the SF form, there could hardly be a better example.

Basic situation: generations before the novel's opening, Earthmen settled Pern, third planet of a golden G-type star; an Earth-like world with a stranger-planet that swings around Pern in a wildly elliptical orbit bringing it close to Pern every two hundred years at perihelion. Centuries later, the colonists of Pern have totally forgotten their Terran origins. They have joined with an indigenous life-form, dragons capable of breathing fire when they chew "firestone" and transform it with their digestive acids into flame producing gases that ignite on contact with oxygen, to battle Threads—airborne spores catapulted off the Red Star stranger-planet at perihelion—which destroy all vegetation when they burrow into Pernese soil. The dragons and humans are telepathic, one-to-one. A specific dragonrider communicates mentally with his dragon. But it has been four hundred years since the last incursion of the Threads, and the memory of the Pernese has grown dim.

All of this is given, quite explicitly, in the introduction to the book. No one should be confused for long.

As the novel begins, we find Pern a world with a semi-feudal culture, split into two distinct societies. The Holds, ruled over by Lords, which raid and conquer one another. And the Weyrs, where dwell the last of the dragonfolk, those who ride the great winged telepathic dragons, and who live by the tithes they extract from the Lords. But in four hundred years, with no sign of Threads, the Lords have almost forgotten the need of keeping the Weyrs stocked with food and supplies, and they rail under the useless tribute paid to a high caste of what seem useless and indolent ex-heroes.

Miss McCaffrey has sketched in all of this preceding background—save for some extremely important explanations which she reveals as she goes along—well in front; an enormous aid in following the line of the plot. (A cautionary note from which should be taken by other writers whose elaborate cosmographies or societies may be clear to *them* when they begin writing, but which far too frequently only emerge out of murkiness and re-readings for an audience that comes to each new world with the eyes of babies.)

Yet for the first half of the novel, very little is done with either the world of Pern or the feudal condition of its natives. The first half of the book is—while not precisely *slow*—terribly measured. (I have heard enough praise for the first section, published in *Analog* as "Weyr Search"—and its nomination for a Hugo bears out the high esteem in which the section is held by the mass readership—to accept that the first portions of the novel may not be plodding for *everyone.* Even so, on strictly craft levels, the "Weyr Search" chapters demand some critical analysis.)

In the first section we meet the ostensible protagonist of the work, the girl, Lessa. I say ostensible, for Miss McCaffrey has the damnable habit of switching viewpoints between Lessa and F'lar, the bronze dragonrider, to the detriment, I feel, of the novel's unity.

Lessa was a child when Lord Fax invaded Ruatha and conquered the Hold, murdering all those of noble blood. By secreting herself in the weyr of the household watch-dragon Lessa was able to retain her life. When Fax left, returning to his home Hold, Lessa emerged and began an existence as a kitchen drudge, cloaking her identity through the use of an ability to "cloud men's minds so they cannot see her" as she really is. With the thought of revenge driving her, Lessa grows to young womanhood, waiting for an opportunity to bring about Fax's death.

The opportunity presents itself when F'lar—on a Search for a new Weyrwoman to meld with a soon-to-hatch queen dragon—finds her. The balance with the first section deals with Lessa's maneuvering of F'lar so he kills Fax, and F'lar's convincing Lessa she should come back to the dragonmen's Weyr to become Weyrwoman. That's all. One would think that with such a brevity of plot-thrusts a richness of detail anent Pern, its special alien nature, the people living there, and the lore of the dragon folk would fill out ninety-one pages. But it doesn't. The feudal background could be compared with invidious results to any of a dozen other science fiction novels, not the least of which would be the hearty offerings of Poul Anderson—whose work this novel resembles in many ways. But where *The High Crusade* or *Three Hearts and Three Lions* manages to convey an extraordinarily rich, one might almost call it heady, savor of times gone by, Miss McCaffrey's scent of the past is thin and almost bland. This should not be. For, stop to consider, not only does she have going for her all the remembered lore and mystique of the *Terran* past against which her Pernese past is paralleled, but she has the benefit of dozens of other SF novels that have dealt with cultures similar in tone to the Pernese. It would seem a not too difficult task to use those intimations, reflections and snippets of minutiae employed with such ease by almost *every* writer in the genre to hint at a richer, fuller background. But Miss McCaffrey does little in this way. The story of Lessa and her revenge could as easily have been written by Sir Walter Scott (though probably not with as much leanness). The language is the stilted, affected "regal" syntax many writers employ when they think they are writing mannered prose.

On this point, then, I would seriously fault Miss McCaffrey's creation. She has not seized, until one-fourth through the novel, a *leitmotif* that most surely makes this an historical work, and a work of importance by way of its explication of the interplay of peoples with their societies and their natural environment.

It is an oversight difficult to understand.

In all fairness, I must note that this richness of detail occurs more regularly in the three-fourths of the novel not yet discussed. But we are never treated to a full merchandising of the wares Miss McCaffrey has built into her world. (I am reminded, as another aside, of the way in which Heinlein has always managed to indicate the greater strangeness of a culture with the most casually dropped-in reference: the first time in a novel, I believe it was in *Beyond This Horizon,* that a character came through a door that ... dilated. And no discussion. Just: "The door dilated." I read across it, and was two lines down before I realized what the image had been that the words had urged forth. A *dilating* door. It didn't open, it *irised*! Dear God, how I knew I was in a future world.)

McCaffrey, with all the past impressions of bad MGM movies and all the implanted lore of every swordplay thriller from Dumas to Sabatini, should have been able to show us her world more colorfully in that first section. Why should she? Because, very simply, for the first fourth of *Dragonflight,* there is something akin to boredom.

It is necessary for a critic to express his opinions, his positions, even his most minor crotchets, early on. In that way, the reader is never in doubt as to the motivations for critical judgments. Herewith, a basic one you may try to remember when considering these criticisms: a writer may have a message, an emotion, a philosophy to impart in his fiction, and these are the most marvelous kind of serendipity. But his first job is to entertain. To inform comes second. To entertain comes first. So, in my view, the single greatest crime a writer can commit is to bore. If a book cannot hold me past the first few pages, I have to struggle to compel myself to go on. (I have been faulted for this narrowness of nature—with good cause, I might add—by writers to letter columns of several fanzines, who have accused me of limited vision, lack of tenacity and outright stupidity. They have also indicated their pity that I've missed some very worthwhile books, most notably *Dune.* I cannot argue with them, I can only report the way the mechanism functions.)

This is not to say that *Dragonflight* as a whole is a bore. Nor even that the first section is *in toto* boring. Only that there is a *tendency* toward boredom in the first ninety-one pages. And in a book as good as this one, I find even the taint of boredom a ghastly presence, possibly all the more noticeable because the book is so good.

Well, then, to what can we attribute this boring tendency in the first section? Partially, as I've indicated, a lack of drawing upon the world in which Lessa lives, for a depth of background that would shore up such a thin plot-development. But this is only the lesser part of the responsibility. The greater share is due to the central topic of this analysis: the "woman's" view.

Unfortunately, most of the failure of this section, due to the "woman's view," cannot be explicated. It is in the nature of tone, of shadow more than reality; my friends on the Strip would say it was all in the "vibes"; I would say vibrations, but that's because I'm on the other side of the Gap, sockittowardsme!

So I can't tell you at this point in space, time and analysis what it is content-wise. But let me go on with the book, and by the time we reach the bottom line, I'll have it for you. Even a critic sometimes has to grope for the proper words: but that's all to the good. It removes from your minds the sureness that we critics are infallible gods, with clear vision. I'm sure that's what you thought.

Parts three and four of the novel appeared in *Analog* (December 1967, January 1968) as "Dragonrider." In the novel they are titled "Dust Fall" and "The Cold Between." Part two (called "Dragonflight" in the novel version) is first published in the Ballantine totality. It concerns itself with an attempt on the part of the Lords of the Holds to wipe the last of the dragonfolk off the face of Pern. They are turned back with what might most generously be termed underwhelming ease. It is not a terribly strong segment, considered in terms of plot, and I can well understand why editor Campbell chose to exclude it from the magazine version. It isn't necessary. Correction: it wasn't necessary for *him*.

In terms of the overall effect the book makes, it is immensely valuable. For in this section we begin to see Miss McCaffrey in her long suit: dealing with the futuristic novel of manners.

In the second section Miss McCaffrey deals with Lessa's gradual growing-into-state at the Weyr. Her training as a Weyrwoman, the relationship she has not only with F'lar—her airborne John Wayne—but more importantly with her great golden queen dragon, Ramoth. In this second section the author begins to dualistically mine her material: both in terms of characterization and in relation of people to the social structures.

It is here that the book finally catches fire. Life pours in as we see F'lar in terms other than as merely a killing machine for Lessa's revenge. We see Lessa for what *she* is as well. Unfortunately, we don't see her the way Miss McCaffrey would have us see her. We are intended to view the telepathic Weyrwoman as a strong-willed, cunning little minx, tipped brimful of the survival stuff. In point of fact she emerges as a silly, vain, cranky adolescent intent on doing precisely the opposite of what everyone asks of her. (And here I find one of those author obfuscations that infuriates me: there is an intricate plan for the future being implemented by F'lar to restore the dragonmen to their former lofty station, in preparation for the arrival of the Threads. To carry the plan through, he needs Lessa's cooperation. But he never tells her what his plan *is*. So she regularly fucks it up, through spite and wrongheaded impetuousness. It makes for some nice plot-complications, and a little artificial conflict, but it could all be avoided if someone just *once* sat down with someone else and said, "Now here's what's going on . . ." But no one does. They avoid telling her the simplest, most logical facts, for no discernible reason in the construct of the plot, but merely because the author needed to advance the story. This is dishonest. It is what Knight calls the "moron plot twist." And the frustrating part of it is that McCaffrey never *needs* to do it! The story works just as well with everyone being informed. Oh well . . .)

I suddenly realize that my objections to elements in the book I consider negative are definitely imparting a feeling that I disliked the book. Odds blood! Nothing could be further from the truth. I *liked* the book. Even admired it in places. The blemishes on its surface rather anger me because it *is* such a rewarding novel. So from this point on, I will praise, not knock. A valentine, from this point on.

The failure of the book (he said, proving himself an instant liar) is in the relationship between F'lar and Lessa. Against a background of the Civil War, Margaret Mitchell managed to tell a coherent and even touching love story between Rhett Butler and Scarlet O'Hara. The enormity of historical events only served to showcase the futility and intensity of their relationship. Anne McCaffrey has attempted the same trick, and failed. When F'lar (who keeps brushing that goddam forelock off his snow-white brow, like someone out of a *True Confession* soaper) gets justifiably angry with Lessa, he doesn't do what any normal man would do . . . belt her or toss her up against a wall, or impress upon her by the force of his (alleged) indomitable personality that she is a jerk and had damned well better shape up before she sacrifices the entire planet to her immature tantrums . . . he shakes her. Not very hard, for she always laughs at him with "teasing vexatiousness" or some other such silly modifier. (I won't go into it here, but Miss McCaffrey is one of the great practitioners of what Blish calls "Said-bookism." People "grunt," "drawl," "breathe," "all but shriek" and ring almost every change short of Mark Clifton-ism or Arthur Zirul-ism, rather than "say" something. It is a bad habit that, once having been pointed out to Miss McCaffrey, should disappear from her later work.)

F'lar is supposed to be a very strong man indeed, but he

acts like a simp where Lessa is concerned.

And that brings us directly, face-to-face with the "woman's" view, what is wrong with the book in the main, and the final explication of the topic at hand.

Anne McCaffrey has taken as her tools the form and content of the most masculine specie of speculative fiction: the hard science adventure novel. There is a complex use of the elements of planetary geography, ecology and inferred astronomy. Added to this is the swashbuckling story-line. And larded on top of all this is the basic love story. Now this is tantamount to juggling a dozen balls all at once. It takes an adept to keep them all in the air. For the most part McCaffrey keeps the spheres spinning. But too frequently the ball representing the person-to-person story falls and hits her on the foot.

Her people don't ring true in terms of the world on which they live. Lessa has undergone privation, torture and utter poverty. Yet at no time does she seem to have been affected by them. It is as if she went through fire and was not touched. F'lar is hellbent on a mission of intricacy and subterfuge to save his world, but he goes about it with the mannered ease of a ribbon clerk. One gets the feeling that he is moving through the story as a marionnette; more manipulated than manipulating.

These become, all too frequently, the stick-figures of the ladies' fiction. They posture and perform at the whim of the author.

The relationship of the man to the woman is in no way recognizable as realistic, not only insofar as *we* relate today, in this time, now . . . but in any terms that we can relate to through the literature of the past. (To cop out and say they are relating as people in the future would relate is a dodge: their circumstances parallel our own, emotionally, and the reference points are in today, therefore a consistency must be maintained or it becomes a case of excusing boredom in a story by saying the author was cleverly trying to describe boredom.)

While I am not saying that McCaffrey should have dealt in terms of cynicism and masculine sweatiness to make her points, I am saying that one cannot hope to make a world of rigor and hardship come to life for what it is, and then populate it with anachronistic Victorian types who do a stately pavanne. The clang of dichotomy deafens, and the book is thereby made infirm.

On the positive side, however, Miss McCaffrey has saved herself in the latter half of the book with great skill and the putting-together of a jigsaw puzzle. Most of the questions asked in the early sections of the book are answered by action rather than description. McCaffrey has a skillful way of showing, not telling.

The book succeeds in great part because of the potency of the world and its dragons as attention-getters. What she lacks in hard-driving emotionalism, she makes up in suddenly revealed plot-twists. We suddenly learn that the dragons can teleport back through time. We learn that Lessa Today was the savior of the world by going back and becoming Lessa Yesterday. We rediscover the past. We find out where the mysteriously disappeared dragonfolk of all the other Weyrs went. It moves rapidly, beginning with part three, and it holds firmly.

This book is a notable property, not only for the sheer enjoyment the latter half provides, but as a talisman for the future. Miss McCaffrey's talent is a very substantial one. She is a writer. That she is—careful with this word—tainted by feminism is something she will either have to rid herself of, or learn to deal with. Other women writers have done it, most particularly Kate Wilhelm and Katherine MacLean. If she can, then what we will have is a humanist Hal Clement, a writer capable of creating the worlds of wonder we have come to expect as a staple of speculative fiction, combined with a nice feel for the male/female relationships those worlds will create.

There are flaws in *Dragonflight,* as I've perhaps belabored, but make no mistake, this is a fascinating novel, filled with color, filled with ideas, filled with the indefinable aroma of a new talent discovering itself.

We await with hope Miss McCaffrey's next offering, and suggest she delve more deeply into the writings of Nathanael West, John D. MacDonald, Jim Thompson and James M. Cain to get a grasp on less butterfly characterizations.

It may be that a woman *can* outdo the muscle-flexers in speculative fiction. One can only observe that C.L. Moore and Leigh Brackett beat Robert E. Howard at his own game, and I watch with great interest as Anne McCaffrey—who is no Becky Thatcher let me tell you—goes after Heinlein and Asimov and Clement. It is a rough arena to choose to fight in, but I suspect the broad has got the moxie to make it.

In any case, we welcome with pleasure her mainstream attack on the hallowed forms of the genre.

There are all too few guerrilla warriors in the jungle these days. If McCaffrey can keep from getting her skirts caught in the underbrush, she may be our next Che Guevera.

THE WHORE WITH A HEART OF IRON PYRITES, OR, WHERE DOES A WRITER GO TO FIND A MAGGIE?

So there was a screening of a new Clint Eastwood film (that turned out to be a genuine off-the-wall downer) and I didn't feel like going alone, so I called Lynda and asked her if she wanted to go and she said yes, and I drove out to Sepulveda (where there were just a *gang* of Wallace stickers everywhere, which made me more than a little twitchy, may I tell you) to pick her up, and her cousin Lane answered the door and let me in and told me Lynda was getting ready, so we sat and chatted till she put herself together. "I, uh, understand you write science fiction," he said. I nodded. "How, uh, how do you get into that?"

Fascinating question. There is no intelligent answer beyond pointless smalltalk, of course. Because it's a dumb question. It's like having someone ask you, how do you get into sex? Obviously, the response is: you just start doing it. Modifying the answer slightly to apply to writing—as opposed to sex, which even the inept can get into—the best you can offer is, "If you have talent, you just start doing it."

Setting aside flippancy, however, one might say you "get into" writing by being incredibly perceptive about people, by observing everything, the smallest details of how people speak and think, how they carry themselves, how they dress, how they compromise themselves, what they think of themselves and others, and how they react in company, how they pursue their goals, how they screw themselves up, what they do to make themselves feel good and in what special ways they unconsciously set about destroying themselves, what effect criticism has on them, how they react to love, what portion of their days is spent in revenge and what portion spent in adjustment to the world around them. . . .

In short, what you say is get to know people, and from your store of amassed knowledge will spring ideas for stories. Because *that* is the answer to the other dumb question asked of writers (usually by people in lecture audiences or by suburban housewives and orthodontists at cocktail parties): "Where do you get your ideas?"

And if you intend to be a writer, you'd better face the fact that you will have these two questions asked of you a million times before they put you down the hole. Because almost *everyone* thinks he can be a writer; most would stop short before they assumed they could be nuclear physicists or concert violinists, but *everyone* thinks he has a great novel in him, if only he had the time to sit down and do the writing. Nonsense, of course; but could you only be a fly on the wall and hear how many nits come up to writers and say, "I've just had a terrific life, really super-interesting, and why don't you write my life, and I'll split all the money with you fifty-fifty," you'd know the core truth of that sad experience.

Because, at bottom, no matter how many sensational ideas you have for stories, you'll never be a writer unless you know people, and you'll never be a writer unless the people in your stories come to life. The best plot-line in the world is merely a series of incidents without living, breathing people scurrying along that line; but conversely, a dud of a story can be arresting if the people are compelling.

Ideally, a writer with talent will meld both into a story that makes you believe and care because the people are real and interesting, and what happens to them is different and fascinating. But if I were denied one or the other, I'd opt for the people over the plot, because it's as William Faulkner said in his Nobel Prize acceptance speech (December 10, 1950): ". . . the problems of the human heart in conflict with itself which alone can make good writing because only that is worth writing about, worth the agony and the sweat."

What I might have said to Lane is, go and live a lot of days and nights, and observe like crazy, and store up a vast knowledge of people, and then simply sit down and start spending *more* days and nights all alone with your typewriter, putting those people down on paper in fresh and fascinating ways. But how do you say that to someone who asked you the question in the first place? If he asked it, chances are good he never will be a writer. It's one of those things a writer knows intuitively. To ask it means the intuition isn't there.

Yet if I'd answered Lane with the secret formula offered above, would he not have followed up with the next stage question: "Where do you find the people you write about?" And that's the same question as "Where do you get your ideas?"

Well, it would take an essay easily as long as this one to *approach* an answer to Lane's other question, but since I'm here, and you're here, why not take a shot at it.

For instance, where did Maggie come from?

Parts of her came from a female named Shawn (who, when I laid a copy of the published story on her and told her she was the model for Maggie, looked at me as though I'd just come up through a trapdoor under a mushroom; she couldn't see herself in the character; which is precisely the way it *should* be; Maggie was born out of Shawn, but Shawn ain't Maggie; nor is Maggie Shawn, if you get what I mean; there are points of similarity, and the general ambience *for me as a creator* is the same, but a creature of my own devising could never be taken from life stick for stick and stone for stone).

But *how* Maggie came to be born maybe possibly perhaps sorta kinda answers the question where stories and characters come from. So I'll tell you how it happened.

I met Shawn in 1963, here in Los Angeles. She was, and is, an extraordinarily beautiful woman with a commanding manner and a sense of self that projects her presence even when she walks into a crowded room. I have seen entire parties of wild revelers fall silent and stare when Shawn enters the room. She dresses elegantly, she's tall, her face is as I described it in the story, and taken in sum she is one of those women whose like you will not encounter twice in ten years.

I have no idea what Shawn *really* does for a living; I am certain she isn't a hooker or a call girl, yet I'm equally as certain she is the sort of woman who would use her uncommon femininity and sensuality to snare a wealthy man, and ride his life for as much, for as long as it was necessary to come away with handfuls of value. But she clearly treasures herself enough not to sell too cheaply. She is the sort of woman—as I see her—about whom Lautrec was speaking when he said, "Women never give their love, they lease it . . . at the very highest rates of interest." Please note the distinction I try to make here: *not* a chippy or a whore, but a woman who uses sex as merely another utensil to achieve her life-goals. The distinction is important, because it goes to the heart of Maggie's characterization. In the story, Maggie is *with* Nuncio, but as she makes perfectly clear to her paramour, she doesn't *belong* to him; she is still her own property. Had I made her one-dimensionally a tart, a piece of meat, I don't think the story would have squeezed the heart of the theme as I believe it now does. These often subtle and tonal distinctions in characterization can make all the difference between drawing a fresh character and merely setting out another cartoon. . . . In this case it would have been a whore with a heart of gold, that stale cliché of 1930s tearjerkers and cheap novels by writers more concerned with establishing their *machismo* than turning the mirror of life in a new way.

But, I wander from my story. To return . . .

I had a physical attraction for Shawn, but it was held in check by a gut reaction to her that I always seem to get in the face of whitewater, whirlpools, and fast currents. We never got down, as they say in the street. And in a strange sort of way we became friends; Shawn as one of those alien totems each of us keep in our world to show us how well-adjusted and "normal" we are; myself as something of a knowledgeable elf who made bright conversation at dull dinners, someone who wakes up alert at any wee hour of the night when the desperate phone calls are made.

One night we got back to her little house and she was pretty well drunk. I carried her into her bedroom, and it was a bedroom precisely like the one I describe in the story, even though I never described it in the story.

(Now what the hell does *that* mean?! Either he described it in the story, or he didn't. You can't have it both ways.

(Wrong. You *can* have it both ways; in fact you've *got* to have it both ways if you want your characterization to work, if you want your people to have the semblance of life. Because—and here's the essence of it—what a writer must strive for is not the journalistic re-creation of life, but verisimilitude, an altered and heightened perception of life that *seems* to be real. In this way a writer can select those elements that work best, seem strongest, make the point most precisely. And in a writer's tool kit the best implement to attain that verisimilitude is a familiarity with the background of the characters. All the unspoken things, all the minute details that need never show up on the printed page but nonetheless live there in shadows, behind the words.

(Shawn's bedroom had flocked wallpaper, blood red and black. A huge bed with an ornate wrought iron headboard. There was sensuality everywhere, in each individual item she had chosen to place in that room. The bathroom was an extension of the bedroom, down to the gold dolphin spigots on the sink and bathtub. In its way it was a toney echo of a posh New Orleans pleasure house, and though there was nothing concrete on which one could fasten to make the comparison, the *totality* was one of . . . of . . . how can I phrase it . . . of *Maggie-ness*. The room was an extension of her needs, her drives, her past, her hopes for the future, her style, and her *façade*.

(I didn't happen to write in a scene that took place in Shawn's bedroom, but that bedroom was there, informing every line of description about Maggie. For me, the physical presence of that bedroom capped my feelings about who Shawn was, and the memory of it hung over me as I wrote the story. And so, without writing in that element of Maggie's backstory, it was *there*, not merely as data but as a pivotal element.)

We could have made it that night, but the wariness I noted earlier led me to cover her with a blanket and to quietly let myself out.

I didn't see Shawn again for two years.

On Thursday, October 7, 1965, I was in Las Vegas and we met again. I'd written (and been rewritten horribly) a film called *The Oscar* for Joseph E. Levine's Embassy Pictures. Though I'd written it for Steve McQueen and Peter Falk, they cast Stephen Boyd and Tony Bennett and to promote Bennett's first (and as it turned out, last) film role, Levine flew the entire cast and crew, as well as publicity cadres, from Hollywood to Vegas, for Bennett's opening at the Riviera Hotel.

146

Now, a brief digression that is no digression at all. People function in the context of their environment; that's such an obvious remark I shouldn't have to make it, but frequently even I am surprised at the *naïveté* of those who want to be writers but ask questions like "Where do you get your ideas," so I'll state it here.

Understanding that statement, you will understand that characterization can be established in terms of setting. That is, one kind of person finds emotional sustenance living in a rural area, another finds it in big cities. A writer can flesh out a character by relating him or her to the scene in which the character functions. It takes a particular kind of person, it seems to me, to prowl successfully in Las Vegas. The Country Mouse couldn't make it, and even the City Rat has some trouble. Because Vegas is neither a city nor a town. It is a cultural artificiality, an unnatural lump in the middle of a desert. A thing that could never have flourished had it not been for greed and shallow dreams and a condition of need in the American Character that demands fulfillment in Disneylands of all sorts. The ambience of Vegas is somehow Lovecraftian to me; dark and evil and glittering with a Borgia smile under that innocent Nevada sun while it leaches all joy and hope from the souls of the world's losers—guys like Kostner, for instance. (As an aside to an aside, maybe it takes the mind of a fantasist to see those qualities in Vegas; I know dozens of people who *live* in Vegas and they tell me of the churches and schools and good living, but I get the creeps every time I get near the place and it took another fantasist, Richard Matheson, to perceive what I perceived in the town, when he wrote the screenplay for *The Night-Stalker;* thereby reassuring me that I wasn't the lone soul who sensed nightmare behind the neon.) And it occurs to me, relating to "characterization," that a highly effective technique for building original characters *vis-à-vis* the special setting in which the character operates, must draw on these subcutaneous vibes given off

147

by the place, whether it be a Harlem tenement or an antebellum mansion in a Louisiana backwash or a gambling casino in Las Vegas. Again, the *intuitions* of the writer must be called into play. You see, it wasn't such a digression, after all.

So. Las Vegas. A special place with a special feeling all its own. A throb of illicit sex, a tension, an undercurrent of danger and excitement, a special sound in the air.

I'd attended Bennett's performance at the Riviera—black tie and tuxedo, lots of lovelies and lots of glitter—and afterward my producers and the rest of the company from *The Oscar* had gone off to do their individual numbers. Some to hustle the showgirls, some to sleep, some to gamble. I was wide awake, though it was after midnight, and so I plonked myself down at a blackjack table and started playing.

Perhaps a half hour had gone by, when I felt a hand on my shoulder. I turned around from the dealer and there was Shawn, looking extravagantly luscious, and suddenly—click!—fitting into the scene so perfectly I realized without even having to think about it, that Shawn was born for Las Vegas and, contrariwise, Vegas had been born for Shawn. According to the old saw, had Las Vegas or Shawn not existed, in fact, they would have had to be invented for one another.

I cashed in my chips. (As a personal note, the character of Kostner is not the Author. Often a motivating force in a character comes from the writer's own personality, but in the case of Kostner, who is a *loser*—in all the deepest life-meanings of that word—I was drawing from other sources. In the story, Kostner loses and loses at the tables. In real life I win constantly. That's what's called, in writing, playing against the Portnoy Syndrome.) We took a walk out to the parking lot. Shawn told me she was working in the line at one of the casinos. Which struck me as odd. She'd never indicated she even knew how to dance, and to dance in one of the chorus lines at the big Vegas hotels, a woman had to be *good*. There are, of course, what they call "statue nudes," who just stand around looking elegant, but I had a niggling feeling Shawn wasn't telling me the truth. She may have been into some convoluted hustle and didn't want me to know. It doesn't matter, really. She told me she was living in Vegas, and why didn't I come home with her.

That was probably the only moment in our relationship during which we might have wound up in bed. And I must confess I was about to say yes. But something was gnawing at the back of my mind; something about Shawn, and Las Vegas, and the night, and its electrical immediacy. I said no, and she got into her car and took off; we'd exchanged the usual vacuous promises to keep in touch.

I stood in the parking lot, trying to let that thought feeding on the back of my brain chew its way to the top. Understand: I was becoming detached from my own reality at that moment. If there is a moment a writer can point to, in an effort to isolate the instant of creativity when a story takes form in his or her head, the moment philosophers have tried to isolate since before the dawn of recorded history, it *must* be moments such as the one I lived through in the parking lot of the Riviera Hotel in Las Vegas. Because *something* was bubbling up, all the unconscious relays were being closed, all the computations were being made, all the file cards of stored data were being processed.

I walked back into the casino, and sat down at the blackjack table. But I didn't bet. I was thinking, and I'd returned, instinctively, to the territory where the dream had been born. The dealer grew annoyed at my taking up space, but he worked around me.

Sounds. It was an amalgam of *sounds* that finally triggered the dream into my conscious mind. The sounds of slot machines clicking, clicking, turning and paying off . . . the sounds of people betting their futures hoping to escape their presents . . . the wheel of fortune . . . the voices of the croupiers and dealers . . .

And it all fitted together.

Shawn. Las Vegas. The insidiousness of gambling machines. The worship of a modern deity personified by chance and the despair brought by the death of luck.

I bolted away from the blackjack table and rushed upstairs.

It is a peculiarity of mine that I travel with my typewriter. Wherever I go, the machine is with me, because I've found there is no predicting when the dreams will hit. The typewriter was waiting, and I tossed off my clothes and started writing. (It is endemic to understanding what follows, to appreciate that frequently I write in the nude. It's no big artistic trip, it's simply a matter of convenience. When I write I frequently pace around and get very physical as the story unfolds. Sometimes I act out the parts and carry on conversations with the characters. So: I was naked and writing, in a Vegas hotel room where the air conditioning was Arctic.)

I've found the hardest part of any story is building the character properly. Usually it has to be done from the kernel out. The kernel being that particular function the character will serve in the plot-line. If it's necessary for a character to perform heavy action, for instance, it would be suicidal to make the physical characteristics inadequate: a cripple, a tubercular, a very short person, an adolescent . . .

If it's necessary for a character to grasp some abstract idea or arrive at some deep philosophical or moral decision, then it would be self-defeating to make the character a lout, or amoral, or so debased that the decisions seem inconsistent with the basic nature of the character . . .

These are rules-of-thumb, naturally. One can achieve fine counterpoint by presenting a cripple with a situation in which he or she must overcome the infirmity to save the day, or, similarly, one can strike a note of humanity if one takes a character who has never had to make fine ethical distinctions and show him or her grappling with the need. But in the main, the rules hold up.

It is also troublesome, sometimes, deciding whether a pivot character should be male or female.

Traditionally in fiction, men have been the viewpoint characters, the saviors, the heroes. I chalk much of that up to male chauvinism. Unconscious sexism.

In the case of "Pretty Maggie Moneyeyes" the problem was even more complex. The viewpoint character could not be Maggie, because of the style and format I'd decided to use, but Maggie had to be the protagonist, the strongest figure in the story. Kostner, to do what he had to do, had to be a loser, a weak man. Such do not make sympathetic viewpoint characters. So I split the viewpoint, integrating Kostner as present time and Maggie as flashback (merging them only in the dream-sequence where Maggie "possesses" Kostner's manhood); but I left wisps of Maggie's character lying about, swirling through Kostner's scenes, so her presence was always center stage.

As I wrote the story, all through that night and into the next day, I became obsessed with Maggie. She was one of the most compelling characters I'd ever created. Actually, it is to laugh: *I* didn't create Maggie, she created *herself.* Which is why I think this is my best story. Because she is *so* right, so fully-fleshed, she speaks to Faulkner's admonition about the only real reason for writing, and she brings to fruition the holiest effort of writing: she becomes a real person. For consider, the greatest books are those in which a single character emerges with that aura of verisimilitude so you never forget him or her. Pip, Huck Finn, Quasimodo, Captain Ahab, Robert Jordon, Jay Gatsby, Ben Reich, Lady Macbeth, Prince Myshkin, Sherlock Holmes, Winston Smith, Tuan Jim, Rima the bird-girl, Sister Carrie, they all burn in the memory, they live on after the book is closed. Long past the time when a reader remembers the intricacies of plot or the niceties of writing style, the *character* stays fixed in the mind. It is as if they lived, they *really* lived, and for the gift of having been brought into contact with a special person like that, there is no fortune a reader can offer the writer in repayment.

But beyond the life I tried to pour into Maggie, there was an energy *she* poured into my writing, forcing me to set her down just so. Thus, again, as many times in the past, I found a character taking over the story. And it seems to me that if a writer is working fine, if the writer is in control of the material, even though he or she may not know in what direction the story is going, the lead character will take charge and help. The stronger a character is fixed in the mind of the creator, the more that character will demand his or her story be told correctly, leading the writer away from one area and into another, taking the plot in directions the writer might never have suspected were inherent in the plot. It is at once a miraculous and a frightening experience.

So strong was Maggie that I wrote and wrote, without conception of time or place or even the needs of the body. And in her way, Maggie did *me* in as well as Kostner. Sitting in that frigid hotel room, I came down with a cold that became acute pneumonia and finally dropped into pleurisy. As best I recall what happened, I collapsed during the second day of writing, was flown back to Los Angeles where I was admitted to a hospital, and woke sometime later yelling for my typewriter so I could complete the story.

The fascinating upshot of what happened is that I do not recall having written whole stretches of the story. The two typographically variant sections immediately after Maggie's heart attack and death were apparently written while I was going into a coma. They are very peculiar sections, indeed: one seems to attempt to describe the moment of death and the other—in the original manuscript—was handwritten in a tiny cribbed hand, the letters printed so small I had to retype the section before it could be submitted to an editor. I think I was trying in my semi-lucid way to describe what it felt like to be a disembodied soul trapped in a slot machine. And if *that* ain't berserk, Spiro Agnew is the Second Coming.

What it all proves, at least to me, is that Maggie is so forceful a personality that in some magic way she wrote her own story. This isn't an isolated happening, incidentally. Almost every good writer I've talked to has told me a similar story; at one or another time in the progress of a certain piece, a character has taken hold and refused to do what the writer thought the character should do. Some have refused to fall in love when ordered, others have refused to die, still others demanded *their* lives were more important than those of the characters the writer had chosen as main viewpoint protagonists. It happens.

Algis Budrys, a writer who used to write some of the best SF ever, told me once, when I was just getting started in the profession, you can't delineate a character by saying he looked just like Cary Grant except he had bigger ears. I remember a story Ayjay wrote, a long time ago, in which the heavy was a bureaucrat who munched candy bars all through a difficult interview with the protagonist. It was a key to the man's nature . . . I don't remember how . . . it's been over sixteen years since I read it . . . but that aspect of the character has stuck with me all this time, though I've forgotten the story it came from. What Ayjay meant about Cary Grant's ears, of course, is that there are no shortcuts to building a character. You have to dig and probe and live some, until you find the elements of humanity necessary to build a specific person to fit a specific story.

Further, you can't *tell* what a character is like; you have to *show* it. The way a character speaks of him- or herself and the truth or lies that reveal themselves when compared against what the character *does;* the way other characters speak of him or her; the way others react to the character—these are the ways in which we come to *see* the personality reveal itself, rather than being *told* this is the way it is, by an omniscient author.

The speech cadences of characters, the way they dress, repeated mannerisms, their smells and the way they carry themselves ... these are all parts of a fully developed sketch, bearing in mind one should tell no more about a character than is necessary for an understanding and identification pursuant to the importance of the character. Chekhov once said, "If, in act one, you display a pistol hanging on the wall, you had better fire it by the end of act two." In other words, don't lard in a glop of irrelevant personality facts if they aren't necessary to the plot or the furtherance of establishing the character as lifelike.

Remember: characters don't exist in a vacuum. They live in context with their era, their place, their past, and the reactions other characters produce in them. They must have an interior consistency. Kate Smith would never get busted smuggling dope. It simply wouldn't play. No one would buy it. Abbie Hoffman would never have a book published by Rod McKuen's Stanyan Press. That's illogical, and a writer has a hard enough time getting readers to suspend disbelief long enough to buy the basic premise of a story—especially an SF story—without throwing an illogical character, operating out of context, into the stew.

I ran into Shawn a couple of months ago at The Farmers' Market. She was looking great. A touch older, perhaps, but tanned and svelte. She was wearing a big eggshell-gray hat that swept down over one eye, and she had just come back from Guatemala or Uruguay or somesuch place.

I told her I was going to write this. She laughed and kissed me on the cheek. "I hope you're not still trying to convince people I'm the model for that terrible person," she said. "No one would believe it!"

Maybe not. But I've got a hunch that somewhere in Guatemala or Uruguay or somesuch place, at this very moment, is a wealthy man who's just a little less wealthy for having run alongside Maggie for a few weeks, and *he* would believe it.

154

VOE DOE
DEE
OH DOE

He introduced me to Scarlatti, Vivaldi, Monteverdi, Buxtehude and hot pizza. I traded him; for Thelonious Monk, Charlie Mingus, the MJQ, Django Reinhardt and Nik-Nik shirts made in Italy. Oh, how I love him.

It cost me over eighty thousand dollars, but I can sit here in my new office wing, built on my house in Los Angeles, and gaze off across my roof not at exposed water pipes and the sternwheeler spatterings of crazed hummingbirds, but a sumptuous expanse of flowering succulents and cacti. *Pseudolobivia Kermesina* gifted me with an enormous pink and scarlet flower just this morning. This evening it was ash-dead. Silverberg built me a roof garden. How I admire and enjoy his books, particularly the sad ones.

I think we'd met before that, but I remember him first as sitting in an easy chair in a convention hotel in Philadelphia in the early Fifties. He wore white bucks. He drank beer from quart bottles. Jesus, I thought he was urbane. Christ, did he have me fooled. He was cool, not urbane. I'm urbane. Now I am, not then I wasn't. I wasn't cool, either. He could fake urbane and be cool, back then; today I can fake cool and be urbane. It's worked out.

Everything (almost) has worked out for Bob and me.

We are luckier than all the rest of you turkeys. That is because we are better than the rest of you turkeys. Voe doe dee oh doe.

He's coming down from Oakland for dinner with me on Sunday, so we talked today. We talk a couple or three times a week. If God hadn't wanted us to keep in such close touch, God wouldn't have given us the money to use long distance telephony so frequently. So we're talking. And I says to him, I says, "Yeah, I've got my reservations about *Star Wars*, too, old chum, but I ain't so dumb: I bought Fox stock when it was at 8; it closed today at 22½."

So Bob says to me, he says, "Sell."

"Nah, not just yet," I say, casually. "There are still lots of terminal acne 'Star Trek' whackos who haven't had their epiphany-conversion to *Star Wars* yet. I'll dump it when it hits 32."

Now Bob knows I don't know shit about stocks—unlike Himself who has a portfolio that would make the shade of J. Paul Getty envious—and he giggles at my punctiliousness. "Next, I buy Trans-America," I say, "because they own United Artists, and when Coppola's *Apocalypse Now* comes out, it'll go through the roof. In fact," I say, "buy some for me through your broker." He knows I'm such a yotz about stocks I don't have a broker, Shearson Hammill having washed their hands of me after that hedge fund debacle. "What's it going for now?"

"About 28," he says. "When I come down Sunday have twenty-eight hundred for me and I'll buy you two hundred shares."

"Okay," I say . . . and there's a moment of silence.

Then we're both laughing, righteously bugfuck, falling down.

"Hey, Bob," I gasp in a breathless voice, "guess what? I

got 2¢ a word from Ziff-Davis today!" And we roar with laughter. Ain't we ludicrous. Ain't we silly. Ain't we beautiful. Just about twenty years ago the both of us were writing our asses off for pennies and hoping to make the rent. Here we sit today in our palaces, talking 200 shares of this and 200 shares of that.

He lived in a magnificent house in New York. Way up in Riverdale, a section of the Bronx that sounds as if it's one of the mythical areas of Ed McBain's 87th Precinct novels, but it isn't. It's New York. The house was sunk to its knees in the ground, some kind of terrific stately manse. It originally belonged to Fiorella La Guardia, "The Little Flower." But there was a bad fire and water damage and Bob had to write a lot of books to rebuild. Then he moved to California. Now he drives a car and raises cacti and he doesn't write any more.

That last part: that's your fault, in large part. I don't want to talk about that. Leave him alone. He's paid his dues.

For a long time, as well as we knew each other, I felt like his idiot kid brother, even though I'm six months older than Himself. He had it all together, had his life ordered, knew the magic vectors and the precise point where the winds of the universe merged. Then one evening he sat on the floor of my old office here at the Los Angeles house, and he cried. If it hadn't been his right to cry, I'd have hugged him and rocked him and said, "It's okay, kiddo, the pain is okay."

And we're closer now. He's been through it with me a few times, and though I'm not much help—just keep telling him to bite the bullet—I'm going through it with him. Did you know he's been my best man at two of my marriages? Or has it been three? No, two; I'm sure it's only two.

I don't think we've ever gone to a movie together in all these years. Lots of dinners, but never a movie. Or roller skating.

There was one night, in Seattle I think, or maybe it was Pittsburgh, when I'd arranged for a "professional courtesy" dinner at a posh restaurant high up on a hill. We did that a lot in the days when we didn't have much money. We'd go to a science fiction convention and, while most fans were slugging down cheeseburgers and soggy fries at the hotel coffee shop, we'd be dining in gourmet splendor at this fabulous dinery or that elegant *boîte*. It wasn't a ripoff, I actually did write a review of every restaurant that ever extended us a free meal. For *Rogue,* or *Topper,* or the Los Angeles *Free Press* or some other magazine. But this one night I'm remembering, there was a mix-up. I think there were six of us. I always passed Bob off as my wine expert, my *sommelier.* I had a date, Bob and Barbara, and two other people, maybe Charlie and Dena Brown. And there was a mix-up. They sent over an expensive bottle of wine with the compliments of the management, and Bob started getting twitchy, asking me, "Are you sure they understand this is on the cuff?" And I kept saying it's cool, leave it to me.

But when the check came, and it came to an empty table, and we were already out in the street, walking down to the car, and the manager came running after us, waving that goddamn check and screaming fraud fraud fraud . . . I went back to explain the way of the world to him . . . and that miserable fink Silverberg ran like a thief. Leaving me to face the wrath of the management. Doo dah.

He wears leather thong sandals. No socks. He has gone California native. I've lived out here for fifteen years and still wear socks and real shoes that cover my toes. I've never heard him sing or whistle; I'm not sure he can do either; isn't that peculiar. He knows the one thing about me I'm afraid to have revealed. I suppose I can trust him with it. He's never yet spilled the beans. Maybe he doesn't know he knows it.

There are scenes in *Nightwings* that can choke your heart. Don't *anybody* tell me he can't write emotionally. And *Thorns* is one of my favorite books. But he likes a lot less of my work than I like of his. That's okay, we're friends.

On my wall I have some framed pictures that remind me of stages of my career, or moments of pleasure. A photo with Steve McQueen and a dune buggy on a 120° day in the high desert out near Thousand Palms. A shot on the set of "Cimarron Strip" with Stuart Whitman. A photo of me with Isaac and Janet at some dinner party where I wore my fabulous $400 chocolate brown velvet tuxedo. And one of Bob and me holding the Hugos we won on the same night. It was his first. He deserved it, but I conned him into believing I had logrolled to sway the vote. I didn't, of course, but it induced him to pay for dinner the next night. Let's see: I paid at Antonio's, he paid at Au Petite Cafe, I paid at Dar Maghreb, he paid at The Rangoon Raquet Club. Hmmm. Hey, Bob, you know your Hugo nomination this year, for *Shadrach in the Furnace*? Well, what's it worth to you if I, uh, er . . .

Here are some things you may not know about Robert Silverberg.

- As second President of Science Fiction Writers of America he was the man who got Sol Cohen of *Amazing Stories* to agree to pay writers for reprints of stories. Until that time, Sol was just filling up magazine after magazine with file stories most of us had gotten a penny-a-word for ten, twenty, thirty years before. Bob made money for many of us. Not much money, but found gold nonetheless.

- There has only been once in all the time he's been eating spicy food that it was too hot even for *him*. At a restaurant called Hunan Taste where we took Leslie Swigart and Stephanie Bernstein, and we asked the wizened Oriental gentleman to "make it as hot as he would for himself" and there we sat, eating, enjoying it enormously, tears of pain rolling down our cheeks.

- He has written about three times as many books as Asimov. Most of them are under other names, but Bob can still sit back with a gentle smile as Ike's publishers, madly driven to the last full decibel, trumpet Isaac's rapid closing on a 200th publication. And while Silgerverb novels have ceased their pullulation, even Creasey or Simenon would welcome him into the fratority of the prolific.

- He does not drink coffee or tea. He does not smoke, and never has. He doesn't like it when you do it around him.

- During the summers of the period 1951-54, he was a camp counselor in West Cupcake, New York and, though it was a coeducational camp, he got laid infrequently.

- He is right-handed. I am left-handed. We are both Jewish.

- This will be the 25th consecutive Worldcon he has attended.

- He has only one discernible scar: on the back of his left hand. He got it in West Cupcake during a water fight when he did a smart thing in a stupid way. It used to be a bright red slash when he lived in New York, but since moving to the more salubrious California climate, it has become very faint.

- And here's one that's *bound* to get some stupid fan bent on insult into trouble: he does not like to be called "Robert," save by one or two people he's known for years who speak the word with overexaggerated officiousness.

None of these obscure facts are particularly interesting. The really good ones I'm keeping for his epitaph, on the theory if you can't speak ill of the dead, don't speak at all.

Bob's writing style is deceptively simple. It is very much his own voice, yet it has reverberations of the classic writers to whom we return for the pleasures of simply reading a good story: Hugo, Dickens, the best of James, Maugham,

Dumas, Guy de Maupassant. It is Art; and because it is Art that functions at a level of expertise and craft perfected over several decades, it seems effortless, oversimplified, like Fred Astaire's dancing or Picasso's pen-and-ink sketches or John Lennon's compositions. It looks as though anyone could do it, that's how simple and easy it is . . . until the attempt is made and the novice falls on his ass.

Because of his parsimoniousness with the language, because of the calculated regimentation of plotting, because of the dispassion with which Bob often unreeled his stories, the casual reader—whose taste has been brutalized too often by cheap pyrotechnics and disingenuous emotionalism—for many years thought of the work of Silverberg as pedestrian. Then, in the Sixties, he eschewed all that, and began writing novels that were awash with poignancy and darkness. Replacing charm, logic. In place of explosiveness, a rational progression of events leading to the emergence of a kind of voracious inevitability. Not cheap gag humor, but wit. Much pain and examination of the subtler aspects of the human condition.

Readers fled in horror.

Silverberg went out on the land and saw the audience he had idealized in his mind and in his Art, and they were demeaning themselves gladly with "sci-fi" and drivelbooks one notch up from comics. With *Star Trek* and *Perry Rhodan* and the blather of functional illiterates. Shaking his head in consternation and dismay, he stopped writing. And he was gone.

He has often been pilloried by the unperceptive for being slick, one who frequently dealt with gimmicks. But in his 1958 story of cannibalism, "The Road to Nightfall," he was already probing at the essence of the human spirit. In "The Man Who Never Forgot" he spoke to the condition of alienation with which we all suffer. "To See the Invisible Man" meant much to its readers; so much, in fact, that it has been widely reprinted in high school text-anthologies; it is a universal story. "Passengers" was an early warning shot in the battle against the Anita Bryants of the world. What is your favorite . . . run off the names:

Nightwings, Going Down Smooth, Tower of Glass, The World Inside, Ishmael in Love, Downward to the Earth, After the Myths Went Home, The Fangs of the Trees, The Feast of St. Dionysus, Son of Man, The Masks of Time . . . my God, how the list goes on. There hasn't been a year for almost two decades that the writer has not had final nominations in two and three categories of Nebula and Hugo awards. Is it any wonder that Barry Malzberg echoes those who know when he calls Silverberg "the best of us all." No, it's no wonder. And he may well be.

And he is gone.

Well, shit, that isn't so. He's alive and *very* well; perhaps weller than he's been in a long time. He lives high in Oakland, dines well, moves around and sees brightly, and his personal life is no less tangled than it ever was, but there may be light at the end of his perceptions. One can only hope. And he's entitled, fer chrissakes! Twenty-some years working behind a typewriter, a body of work most writers couldn't parallel for quality and mass if they worked night and day for fifty years, a contribution to our cultural self-awareness that few other fantasists can equal . . . he's *done* it. He's entitled to stop, or rest, or pack it in entirely, without rancor, without being chastised. The gift has been given; accept it without greedily demanding more. He's entitled. To live his life as he chooses. The work, once written, belongs to the reader. The writer belongs to himself.

Peace and time are commodities we all find in short supply. Bob has decided to take his full measure. He's entitled.

Anybody messes with him has to go through me.

And the one thing I am, that Siblerverg ain't, is mean.

He was naked beside the pool. So were the ladies. I had white ducks on. I didn't want to make him feel inadequate. It was the day before New Years Eve. The annual Terry & Carol Carr Eve party, to be followed by the annual New Years Day party of the Silverbergs. I was staying in the guest bedroom with the water bed. We were beside the pool, eat your heart out Kalamazoo and New York and Pittsburgh. End of December, beside the pool. Voe doe dee oh doe.

"Bob, take a look at this story."

"Not now, I'm being sybaritic."

"C'mon, man, just read the goddam thing. I know all the stuff is here, but it's gone and went wonky on me. It doesn't sing."

"It doesn't soar?"

"It doesn't swell with pride."

"It just lies there."

"Sucks is, I believe, the proper terminology. Take a look, willya. Tell me what I can do with it."

He read it. Then he held it over the water with thumb and forefinger. "This is what you should do with it."

He dropped it. On the poolside. I went red with anger. Cannot remember when I've been angrier. I grabbed it up and went to the guest bedroom where my typewriter was set up. I'd been working on that story for two years. That miserable sonofabitch! I'll show him!

I wrote all through the day, part of that night; started again the next day with the TV in the guest bedroom blaring the Rose Bowl behind me, with Terry and a dozen other partygoers yelling and drinking and in no way interfering with my concentration.

I reworked the story, snipped apart the sections, rewrote whole episodes, added eight thousand words, finished it the next day. He read it again.

"Not bad," he said. He isn't that high on most of my work.

"It's bloody dynamite," I said, with touching humility.

"Wrong. It's still wonky."

"It's a classic. It'll win a Hugo."

"No way."

The story was "The Deathbird." Eat your heart out Silverbug.

I never had a brother. I have a sister, but with only two moments of pardonable insanity when I forgot how much I disliked her, I haven't spoken to her in eleven years. But if I'd had a brother, he wouldn't have been like Silverberg. Bob and I are too different; very few points of similarity. Yet we are linked. Don't ask me why, don't ask me how. It just is. He doesn't know it, but he's the executor of my estate. If I went tomorrow, I'd go secure in the knowledge that Bob would tend to every little detail of my demise. He'd grumble about it, and think ill of me for inconveniencing him by being hit by a truck or getting myself defenestrated, but he'd do it. Ours is a peculiar and disparate friendship, almost a quarter of a century concretized. But we are so dissimilar that I sometimes wonder what it is we have in common. Clearly, what we have in common, is each other.

In repose, his face resembles a Quechuan stele of the sleeping philosopher-soldier, something carved from the black rock of the steep slopes of the Cordilleras. His walk is easy; neither reminiscent of the cat nor of the rolling gait of the sailor, but loosely from the hips and the lower back. A textbook example of the laughter being primarily in the eyes; the mouth is often questionable. His lips are thicker than might be considered esthetically correct for the face. He has small ears. I remember him before the beard.

Women tell me he is good in bed. I think he is probably even better with women out of bed. That is a terrific thing to be able to say.

Politically, he would like to be more conservative than he is permitted to be, because of his constant exposure to those of us, his friends, who are wild-eyed radicals and knee-jerk liberals. I'm sure it causes him difficulty. He over-intellectualizes too much sometimes. That is, no doubt, because he is an intellectual. He is also an elitist, but is too smart to flaunt it. His manner is quiet, and so his elitism seems acceptably patriarchal and exanimous.

He seldom uses coarse language. He keeps cats.

His work will be read and admired fifty years from now. I'd make book on it.

Appreciation? How do I express appreciation for a man who has been part of my life since the days through which we marched as fans, he with his magazine *Spaceship,* me with *Dimensions*?

He wrote an appreciation of me for a recent issue of *The Magazine of Fantasy & Science Fiction* that ended with a sentence I found making me cry. Not bawling, you understand, just sort of welling up a bit. There was love and bemusement and tolerance and amazement and frustration in that last sentence, and it was a genuine treasure.

If all of the above emotions and attitudes toward him, on my part, don't surface in this "appreciation," then either you as reader or I as writer failed in doing our job.

But for a parting shot, I'm forced to go to another writer for splendid words. It is a piece of an article about film director Sam Peckinpah, written by one of my few friends who is an actor: Robert Culp. You may not have known that Bob Culp is a brilliant writer, but to inform your awareness, here is this snippet of appreciation, written when Culp and Peckinpah were on good terms. I've been saving it for myself. If I could have anything ever said about anyone, said about me, as my epitaph, I would want it to be something like this.

It wasn't written about Silverberg, but you'll allow for the discrepancies, because the tone and the substance go right to the heart of my feelings about Silverberg.

"The similarities in character between Peckinpah and [John] Ford are not exactly lost on those who know them. He *is* Ford, come again just as mean, a little more mad, a little angrier, a little more vulnerable, perhaps a little more valuable to the people around him now, since he is absolutely the last of the breed. With him the line runs out. He is not the technical master of the form that Ford was, but his vision is greater and he is bolder, infinitely more reckless and self-destructive, and as a consequence very precious since he will be with us only a short time. And the body of his work will be smaller. It is very difficult for him to, in his incessant phrase, 'just get it on!' It costs him more to get the job done than any of the rest of us, and there's only so much currency, only so many feet and inches of entrail. [Robert Silverberg] is all alone just like the rest of us. Except that he knows it. He knows how terribly cold it is out there and he cannot come in. But he sends messages."

This appreciation is available in mono and compatible eight-track stereo. Voe doe dee oh doe.

HARDCOVER

It had been under the burned-out house. Richie was quite certain it was the last one. For all he knew it might have been the first one. But something singular, of that he was certain. It was the only one he had ever seen, and of that he was sure.

Book. The word was one of those scratched on privy walls and he knew it well. "Johnny reads books," the walls read, or "Alice does it reading a book," or if they disliked someone: "Bookworm Burris." So the word wasn't unknown to him.

Richie had been going through the rubble of the charred building, kicking aimlessly at clods of mud and the dirt streaked chips that had been furniture. He wished wildly for a miracle so that his goddam home would be smashed flat or something. That goddam father of his was just skirting the line of treason, and Richie was scared white thinking what might happen were the PeepToms to get wind of it. Richie was seriously considering turning his old man over to the Cartel Cops and getting a reward, as well as relieving the tension, when he kicked over the rotting boards and saw book.

It was book. It was last book. Richie knew it was last book because he got around. He was a member of the Sage Street Muckers and an Advance Guard of the 4th Section Regimental Knockabouts. He got around, and no one—absolutely *no* one—had ever mentioned seeing a book. Even though he was thirteen, Richie had experienced thrills and sins an earlier world never even knew existed.

Richie made sure no one saw him pick up book. He bent quickly, shoved it under his jumper, hauled himself over the fence at the end of the empty lot, scurried through a maze of alleys and came out on the hill overlooking the Tube House.

Just thirteen, but he knew the thrill of a forbidden possession. It was book and by Chrize he was gonna read it.

Back of the Tube House, where the commuter-tubes began their runs every half-hour, he snuggled down in the dirt of the hill and looked at book.

His world outside, back around the other side of the Tube House, would have been more than shocked had they seen Richie looking at book. They were rather strict these days about such things. Gang fights with glass hooks on the ends of a five foot pole. Okay. Seduction of the little girl with the bows in her hair as initiation to the TV Non-Virgin Club. Okay. Book. Uh-uh.

Too many people found other ways to think about the things they were supposed to think when they read book. Then it cost the Cartel more to put them back in line, which in turn got Government mad at Cartel, which made Cartel angry, and cut off the good things they could provide, like TV sets and jelly apples and scented kitchen cleanser, and all manner of wonderful—necessary—things.

So book was out.

But Richie had come up with book, and he was goddamned if he wasn't going to read it. Wait'll the next meeting of the Muckers. He'd rack 'em and swow 'em! Man, they'd plow when they eared his find. Man, he was a topboy with *this*. So Richie read book.

He opened the warped and matted cover and looked at the title. It made no sense to him. Such words were gibberish. But Richie was determined to indulge in what he knew to be a sin.

He bent his head, squinted his deep-hued eyes and ran dirty hands through dandruffed blonde hair. The more he read, the more he was embroiled by the senselessness of the thing. What did this mean? What was a . . . *what* was it?

The boy closed the back cover of the book, having skipped much, but still following a twisting passage through the pages of the volume. There was no comprehension.

Ah, to hell with it! Even if he didn't know what the hell it was all about, still he had read it, and wait till the Muckers heard about this. Man, it was top-top secret, and if it got out there'd be real heaps to clean!

The Muckers met on a Wednesday night, and Richie had two hours of school three days a week, and Wednesday was one of them. So he was compelled to keep the news of his find in back of his eyes, tied up in a small sack in his mind, and wait.

The school was a big thing. It reared up in the center of Town and was hardly ever used. Tardiness and absenteeism were no longer evils, they were mainstays. But Richie got a large-charge out of going to that queero school to hear that zagnut of a teach ask them questions. Teach wasn't a bad sort even if he was a demoted PeepTom. They'd demoted him from Section A of the PeepToms for missing an ex-college prof that had lived right in his own house-block, and he'd missed him completely. So now teach was PeepTom of Town School, and Richie liked to listen to the jerko questions he popped.

So Richie always went to school. He was never tardy and never missed a day. He sat in the best seat, way in the corner at the back, and looked at the rest of the kids with their knives (carving the names of their clubs in the desktops) and their rubber-bands (stick a sliver of coke bottle glass in and shoot *that,* man, that's *real* cool!) and watched them carefully, till teach asked a question.

Oh, teach asked some whingers, he did. Like, "When was the last pre-Cartel government purged? Chollie?" And Chollie would answer in his squeaky voice, "Who the hell gives a muckin' damn, teach?" And teach would answer, "Very good, Chollie." Or he'd ask, "Who was the biggest traitor of pre-Cartel government? Herb?" And Herb would spit once at Jenny in the seat next to him and lisp, "Which-ya want, Jawge Washington or my old man? They got *him* in '85."

The schoolroom would rock with laughter and teach would snicker and say, "No, Washington will do. Thanks, Herb."

It was Wednesday and teach was up front with his earphones on, peeping for whispers that might give him a clue to something that might get him re-instated in Section A.

Then came the first question.

Richie wasn't listening. He was mulling over book. There hadn't been much in it he'd understood, but one phrase had stuck with him.

Teach asked, "Where is the capitol of our Great and Glorious Democracy located? Richie?"

Richie's mind muttered to itself. He said what was in his mind. He shouldn't have.

"Twas Brilling, and the slithey toves did gyre and gimble in the wabe . . ." Then he caught himself. "Uh, what the muck ya wanna know for, ya lost or somethin'?"

But the damage had been done. The class's collective necks were twisted and craned at him. Teach stood with his mouth open. "Very, uh, very good, Richie. Excuse me a moment students, I'll be right back." He bolted from the room, while Richie sat and sweated cold.

What had he said. What?

Ten minutes later they came in through the classroom door. The big men with the black suits, skin tight.

Richie leaped up on his seat, backing off it onto the floor, against the wall, "No, ferchrissakes; lemme alone."

They took him by the arms, above the elbow, and carried him from the room, kicking, screaming, muttering gibberish that the other students could not understand:

"You are old father William, the young man said . . ."

Pretty soon, even that faded down the tiled halls, and they went back to spitting at each other.

A WALK AROUND THE BLOCK

Nighttime in Yancey was a velvet cold thing. The night dropped out of the sky like soft-spun candy and draped itself about my shoulders.

I hunched over, shoved my hands deeper into my pockets—unconsciously gripping the ring of keys tighter—and kept walking.

My late evening constitutional or *else,* I muttered inside my head. Doctor's orders, doctor's orders. The monotony of the phrase was a depressant to my ego. Nothing is more odious than doing something pleasant that is unpleasant because you are forced to do it. If you get what I mean. What I mean is—Oh, just forget it. It doesn't really matter. Just verbalizing again.

Yancey stood out as an irregularly-marked line of building tops in black against the light black of the night. Every fifteen feet or so the naked yellow unwink of a street lamp flared up the darkness for a moment, then faded into a back-there-behind-me of non-existence.

Boring. This whole constitutional.

But then, I conjectured, isn't everything basically boring? Isn't life itself merely a game that has been played and played and played again with unfailing sameness? There can be only one real ending for the game, and why we persist in taking a whirl at it when we're pre-destined to lose is beyond me. Which is what got me wondering about God and all. Why?

Why what? That's just *it*! Why a God? Berkeley contended (not too incorrectly I might assure you) that we are all figments of the imagination insofar as we exist. None of this "we are thoughts in the synapses of a greater god" routine, but that actually a thing didn't exist if we couldn't see it, etcetera, because it didn't exist in our frame of reference.

Now you can laugh like Hell at that, but just for the sheer kicks of it I decided I'd try out an extension of Berkeley's theory. Ah, ah, ah, don't quirk up the corners of your lips. If you were walking along the dull, deserted rim of the world on Farrell Street at three in the morning, you'd think of something stupid to do, too. You might break windows though. *I* was merely suppositioning. There *is* such a word—isn't there? At any rate, I decided I was going to will something out of existence.

I turned off Farrell onto Causeway Boulevard and stopped for a moment near the corner to light a cigarette, striking the match off the fire alarm box. The click of my heels as I resumed walking followed behind me like a flock of timid grasshoppers. What should I will out of existence? Right then I almost decided it was all poppycock for myself to be doing such childishness and nearly dropped the whole thing as a bad chain of thought. But for some unaccountable reason I persisted. I would will my street out of existence. Not the whole thing, you understand. Just the street and both sidewalks all the distance from Emery Road to Kensington Court, including fire plugs, street lights, gutters, grass peeping up through cement and anything or anyone who happened to be on them at the time. Merciless, wasn't I?

Well it was more fun that fact when I suppositioned it. I cut through the empty lot that bordered the Causeway and Menlo Park Avenue and took up the stride once again. Here was I, the thought lit in my mind for an instant, a man only fifty-two years old, almost in my prime, and about to be cut down by a cardiac condition. I snickered, tossing my head. Tall enough, handsome enough—you'd be surprised how many barmaids give me the eye—and actually wealthy enough, though Lord knows those taxes will cut it to nothing if that Renmoro Steel proposition doesn't go through next week. Have to call Kemp in Chicago on that tomorrow. Make a note of it. Mmmm. And who am I to be making references to the Good Lord? Here I am trying to prove he doesn't exist. Oh well . . .

Now let's get right to it with a will. Concentrate. The street in front of your house does not exist. It is gone. Vanished. It never existed it does not exist it will never exist it is gone. Kaput! What is gone? Something that was in front of your house. But there is nothing in front of your house. (Now you're getting it—that's the proper attitude for willing things out of existence!) Something which never existed is no longer there where it never was. It is gone as completely as Angkor Wat. As completely as the Lost Tribes of Someone-or-other. Have to look that up one of these days. It is gone. Gone. Disappeared. Evaporated.

I was beginning to believe it myself now. I could picture the expanse, running right up to the edge of my front lawn, as a complete total nothing. Funny, but it was the first time in my life I had been able to imagine Nothing. You know how you concentrate everything you have, when you are a little kid, to try and imagine what's outside the universe. Try to imagine Nothing. I never could, till I tried to imagine that street gone. And it worked, it was a huge bottomless hole in the fiber of space that signified eternal and unchanging Nothing. It was a hole in space. It was black Black. I could see it in my mind's retina. Nothing.

I was almost to the corner of Menlo Park and Emery Road. Then it was a short walk step-on-a-crack-break-your-mother's-back to the expanse of Maple Avenue, my street, which ran into Kensington Court. Which in turn was perpendicular to Farrell. Once around the cold, chilly velvet dark block to satisfy some stupid doctor. Maple to Kensington to Farrell to the Causeway. Down the Causeway through the empty lot onto Menlo Park. Menlo Park to Emery Road and Emery half way up the block to my house. Except there *was* no street after Emery. Emery was a solid concrete and hardtop asphalt roadway with cars zip-zipping across it, but a black Absence after that where Maple should have been. I wasn't suppositioning, that was the way it was. There just wasn't any street there. And for good measure I lopped off the empty yard that was on the corner of Emery and where Maple used to be. It was right next door to my house and I'd never liked it. No one wanted to build on it. Uneven terrain or soft ground or somesuch ridiculousness.

I was coming to the corner of Emery Road. My feet hurt from the walk. The smoke from the cigarette went whipping away in the faint breeze and my foot caught momentarily in the cuff of my pant leg as I walked. How nice it would be to have no cars coughing up Maple. No pedestrians. No street. Just the cliff with the sea behind and below it, up to the edge of my lot behind my house, with Emery running off parallel with the cliff out of town. Quiet.

I turned the corner at Emery and took a step toward my house.

Now I'm not blaming Berkeley. He was theorizing a helluva long while before I was born. And I'm not blaming you fellows from the fire department because they aren't long enough, but goddam it, how do I get across that chasm to my house? I think I left the bathtub running!

HARLAN ELLISON NONFICTION CHECKLIST

This Checklist intends to set out briefly the details of non-fiction books by Harlan Ellison, and to note briefly the *first* publication only of all of his published non-fiction short pieces, including essays, articles, fanzines edited, introductions and afterwords to his own and others' books and short pieces, reviews of all kinds, published letters, and interviews. This is a companion Checklist to that published in the "Special Harlan Ellison Issue" of *The Magazine of Fantasy & Science Fiction,* July 1977, which emphasized first publications of fiction. Please note that this is complete to the best of my knowledge. If you know of other articles, reviews, letters, or interviews, especially in fanzines, please let me know about them at P.O. Box 14671, Long Beach, California 90814. Thank you, LKS. 15 May 1978

Abbreviations. Magazines (where full title is not used): *Adam - Adam Monthly Magazine; B&G - Blue & Gold* [East High School, Cleveland], *F&SF - Magazine of Fantasy & Science Fiction; ItT - Inside the Turret* [Elizabethtown,

KY]; *Kt - Knight Magazine; LA - Los Angeles Magazine; LAFP - Los Angeles Free Press; LAT - Los Angeles Times; MW - Man's Way; Psy - Psychotic; SFR - Science Fiction Review; SFWAB - Bulletin of the Science Fiction Writers of America; Sundial* [Ohio State U.]; *WD - Writer's Digest.* Other abbreviations: apa - also published as; (f) after title of periodical indicates an SF fan magazine, or fanzine; NAL - New American Library.

NON-FICTION BOOKS

Information is given in this order: *Title* (place: Publisher, Date. Pages. Publisher's Number/Series, if any Format Price Number of printings Other pertinent information) Note on contents.

Memos from Purgatory: two journeys of our times (Evanston, IL: Regency, 1961. 160 p. #RB102 paper $0.50 1 ptg) (Reseda, CA: Powell, 1969. 207 p. #PP154 paper $0.95 1 ptg) (New York: Pyramid, 1975. 204 p. #V3706/Pyramid Ellison Series #3 paper $1.25 2 ptgs) (Canadian edition: New York: Pyramid, 1975. 204 p. #V3706/Pyramid Ellison Series #3 paper $1.25 1 ptg Verso of title page: Printed in Canada) (New York: Jove/HBJ, 1977. 204 p. #A4608/Harlan Ellison, 3 paper $1.50 1 ptg) Autobiography. The Regency edition begins with a Message from the Sponsor and a Prologue; the Powell edition adds an introduction: Memo 69; and the Pyramid, both American and Canadian, and the Jove/HBJ editions, add an introduction: Memo 75.

The Glass Teat: essays of opinion on the subject of television (New York: Ace, 1970. 318 p. #29350 paper $1.25 1 ptg) (New York: Pyramid, 1975. 319 p. #V3701/Harlan Ellison Series #1 paper $1.25 2 ptgs) (Canadian edition: New York: Pyramid, 1975. 319 p. #V3701/Harlan Ellison Series #1 paper $1.25 1 ptg Verso of title page: Printed in Canada) (New York: Jove/HBJ, 1977. 319 p. #A3701/Harlan Ellison, 1 paper $1.50 1 ptg) Essays from the *Los Angeles Free Press.* The Ace edition begins with: 23"

Worth of Introduction; the Pyramid, both American and Canadian, and the Jove/HBJ editions add a new introduction: The Glass Teat Revisited: A Supplementary Introduction.

The Other Glass Teat: further essays of opinion on television (New York: Pyramid, 1975. 397 p. #A3791/Pyramid Ellison #5 paper $1.50 3 ptgs) (Canadian edition: New York: Pyramid, 1975. 397 p. #A3791/Pyramid Ellison #5 paper $1.50 1 ptg Verso of title page: Printed in Canada) Essays from the *Los Angeles Free Press* and *Rolling Stone,* with an introduction: Days of Blood and Sorrow.

FANZINES EDITED

During his early career as a fan, Harlan edited and published a number of fanzines to which he contributed editorials, articles, reviews, responses to letters, stories, and poems. The following list gives the *Title,* Volume number (Issue number), and Date for each issue edited by him, plus an occasional comment.

The Bulletin of the Cleveland Science Fiction Society, 2 (1), March 16, 1952; 2 (2; issue 13), March 30, 1952; 2 (3; issue 14), April 1952; 2 (4; issue 15), May 1952; which became:

Science Fantasy Bulletin, formerly the *Bulletin of the Cleveland Science Fiction Society,* 2 (5; issue 16), June 1952; 1 (6), July 1952; 1 (7), August 1952; 1 (8), September 1952; 1 (9), October 1952; 1 (10), November 1952; 1 (11), December 1952; 1 (12), January 1953; 2 (1; issue 13), March 1953; which became:

Dimensions (formerly *Science Fantasy Bulletin*), #14, May-June 1954; 2 (3; issue 15), August-October 1954

Vector, #1 [1952]. One-shot edited with Jim Schreiber

Piddling and Diddling, [1953]. One-shot edited with Lynn A. Hickman

Ellison Wonderland, 1 (1), Fall 1953, *Seventh Fandom Amateur Press Association* [7APA] *Mailing* #1, November 1953, accompanied by *Message to the Accumulated Membership* [membership list and table of contents for Mailing #1]; 1 (2), Winter 1953, *7APA Mailing* #2 [1953-54]; 1 (3), Spring 1954, *7APA Mailing* #3, Spring 1954

ARTICLES, ESSAYS AND OTHER PROSE PIECES

Only first publication is noted. For periodical contributions is given: Article title, *Periodical title,* and Date or Volume and issue numbers and year; for book contributions: Article title, *Book title,* Editor (Place: Publisher, Date). Other published titles are noted, as are pseudonyms used on first publication.

Adam's Bachelor Test for Hipness. *Adam* 3/67

Agents and Bedfellows [participant]. *Proceedings of the Day Program and* [Science Fiction Writers of America] *Nebula Awards Banquet: 1970* ed. G. Benford (Philadelphia: Terminus, Owlswick & Ft. Mudge Electrick Street Railway Gazette, 1970?)

The Agony and the Ecstasy [column]. *Confidential* 9/68, 11/68, 12/68, 1/69

Alicia Lornlove Speaks. *The New Nu News* [Newsletter of the Nu Chapter of Zeta Beta Tau], 10/31/53

The American Male: His Systematic Castration. *Kt* 3/67

Armor School Celebrates 17th Birthday. *ItT* 9/29/57

As "Amahl" Speeds Towards Show Day. *ItT* 12/5/58

Astigmatism and Assassination: Television Then and Now. *Sundial,* 5/54

The Battle of Lake Erie. *Battle Cry* 4/57

Big H-37 Choppers Arrive for Post Duty. *ItT* 12/19/58

Black Thoughts. *SFR* (f) 4/69 (apa: Blood/Thoughts; Dark/Thoughts)

A Brawler's Guide to Los Angeles. *LA* 2/67

Café Ellison Diabolique. *Cooking Out of This World,* ed. A. McCaffrey (NY: Ballantine, 1973)

Camp Lejune Marines Ride Knox Tanks. *ItT* 11/29/57

Candid Confessions of a General's Driver. *ItT* 9/13/57

Captain Charisma Strikes Again. *LAFP* 5/9-15/69

The Case for Our College Bohemians, as Robert Courtney. *Rogue* 8/59 (apa: The College Bohemian)

Celebrities Speak Out on Porn [contributor]. *Hustler* 4/77

Child Soprano Sings Difficult Opera Score. *ItT* 11/14/58

Coffee Houses are Cabarets, Police Say, Owners Deny It. *Village Voice* 9/1/60

Comic of the Absurd. *All in Color for a Dime,* ed. D. Lupoff & D. Thompson (New Rochelle, NY: Arlington House, 1970)

The Common Man: The Common Enemy. *Kt* 4/70

Confessions of a Park Avenue Gigolo [Anonymous]. *MW* 5/56

Congratulations of SF-Magazines 200th Issue. *SF* [Japanese *F&SF*] 7/75

Controversy: Sharpest Sword of the Paperback Novelist. *WD* 1/63

The Credo of the Creator. *WDS* [Writer's Digest School] *Forum* Winter 73

Criticism: Who Needs It? [contributor]. (np: Science Fiction Writers of America, 1968)

The Current State of SF; The New Wave; My Own Contribution. *Stella Nova* (apa: *Contemporary Science Fiction Authors*), ed. R. Reginald (LA: Unicorn Press, 1970)

The D-B Symposium [contributor]. *Double-Bill* (f)

The Dame Hollywood Can't Tame [Anonymous]. *Male Life* 5/56

Dangerous Gism [contributor]. *Citadel* (f) 1976

Darkness in Magic Caverns. *AFI* [American Film Institute] *Report* 5/73

Defeating the Green Slime. *SFWAB* 1/76

Do You Have a Restless Urge to Write? [with Edward Bryant & James Sutherland]. *The SFWA Handbook,* ed. Mildred Downey Broxon (np: Science Fiction Writers of America, 1976)

Down the Rabbit Hole to TV Land. *Cad* 9/67

Dreamers on the Barricades. *Clarion: An Anthology of Speculative Fiction and Criticism from the Clarion Writers' Workshop,* ed. Robin Scott Wilson (NY: NAL, 1971)

Dreamsellers. *KWest*con Program Book* (Kalamazoo, MI: KWest*con, 1974)

Editorial: A Note from the January Editor. *Sundial* 1/55

Edward G. Robinson: The Face at 72. *Cinema* 7-8/65

Ellison on Ellison. *Lunacon - 1973* [program book] (NY: Lunacon, 1973)

Ellison Speaks . . . Prompted by Paul Walker. *LUNA Monthly* (f) 3/73

The Face of Our Times [Anonymous]. *Rogue* 3/60

The Fan Artist: Scribbler in Disguise? *Sol* (f) 8/52

Fantasies of the Famous! [contributor]. *Playgirl* 7/77

Father of Five Calls for Help, Blood Needed. *ItT* 12/19/58

A Few (Hopefully Final) Words on "The New Wave." *Science Fiction: The Academic Awakening,* ed. W.E. McNelly (Shreveport, LA: College English Assn, 1974)

The Fine Art of the 15¢ Pick-up, as Cordwainer Bird. *Adam* 7 (11) 1963

First Run Interviews with Famous Men of the Times. *Sundial* 2/54

Five Lies About Southern Women, as Harlan White. *MW* 10/56

Fort Knox Has Its Own Seer in Pvt. Taylor. *ItT* 10/31/58

Getting Hollywood's Head Straight. *Kt* 3/70

Getting Stiffed. *Torcon 2 Programme Book* (Toronto: Torcon 2, 31st World SF Convention, 1973)

Girls Attend French Legion of Honor School. *ItT* 1/24/58

The Girls of L.A. and Where to Find Them. *Kt* 9/67

The Glass Teat [column]. *LAFP* 10/4-10/68 - 3/26-4/8/71 and *Rolling Stone. The Los Angeles Flyer* 5/11/72 & 5/25/72 (Columns through 1/30/70 reprinted in *The Glass Teat* (NY: Ace, 1970), those after 2/13/70 in *The Other Glass Teat* (NY: Pyramid, 1975))

Goodbye, Gypsy.*Kt* 8/72

Good-bye to the Girl of Easy Virtue. *Kt* 7/67

Grumps That Go Boomp! in the Night. *Cad* 1/67

Hans Stefan Santesson: 1914-1975. *Locus* (f) 3/15/75

Harlan Ellison Hornbook. *LAFP* 10/27-9 [sic, 11]/5/72 - 7/20-30/73; *LA Weekly News* 8/10-17/73 - 12/21-28/73; *Saint Louis Literary Supplement,* 11/76 - 6-7/77

Harlan Ellison Unmasks the Eagle (or Does He?) *The Staff* 2/16-22/73

Harlan Ellison's Guest of Honor Speech at the Ozarkon III. *Sirruish* (f) 8/68

Harlan Ellison's Response to William Rupp's review of *Basilisk*. *Dreadnought* (f) Spring 73

Harlan Ellison's Watching: A Column of Comment on the Visual Media. *Cosmos* 11/77

He Set the Tone. *Speculation* (f) 9-10/69

Horsin' Around with Hamlet [Anonymous]. *MW* 4/56

Hot Tricks for Cold Weather, as Ellis Hart. *Rugged* 4/57

How Girl Gangs Fight and Love. *Rage* 4/57

"How I Survived the Great Videotape Matchmaker." *LA* 2/78

How You Stupidly Blew Fifteen Million Dollars a Week, Avoided Having an Adenoid-Shaped Swimming Pool in Your Back Yard, Missed the Opportunity to Have a Mutually Destructive Love Affair with Clint Eastwood and/or Raquel Welch, and Otherwise Pissed Me Off. *Algol*   Spring 78 (Resignation speech from SFWA)

I Hitch-hike for a Living, as Al Maddern. *Men's Digest* 10/59 (apa: Hitchhiking Can Be Suicide)

I Raped Freedom in Budapest, by Jaroslav Milanyov as told to HE. *Battle Cry* 8/57

In Memorium: Gerald Kersh. *Nebula Award Stories Four,* ed. P. Anderson (NY: Doubleday, 1969)

The 'Incident' Revisited. *Psy* (f) 9-10/54

The Jolly Executioners. *Rogue* 9/59

Kicking the Hobbit; or, Why Do Science Fiction Fans Have Fur on Their Feets? *FM & Fine Arts* 7/68

Kley's Creatures [Anonymous]. *Rogue* 1/61

The Lemming Factory; or, How Daisy Jack Found the Factory Had Swallowed His Quicksand People. *LA* 10/67

A Letter to an Anthologist. *The SFWA Handbook,* ed. M.D. Broxon (np: Science Fiction Writers of America, 1976)

Living with Troll Blood: Some Brief Thoughts on Being a Fantasist. *SFWAB* Fall 74

The Long Walk [column] (with Windi Flightner). *Sundial* 10/54, 11/54, 12/54, 1/55

McKie Course Gives Battlefield Flavor. *ItT* 10/18/57

The Magnifying Glass [column]. *B&G* 10/10/51 - 10/8/52

Make It an "L" and It's Luck, as Cordwainer Bird. *Kt* 11/67

March to Montgomery. *Kt* 9/65

Mr. Smith & the Special Spark: An Appreciation. *A Portfolio of Illustrations by Dennis Smith,* ed. Bjo Trimble (Evergreen, CO: Opar Press, 1969)

The Most Unforgettable Silverberg I Ever Met. *Xenium* (f) 12/74

Muddy Thinking in Supermanland. *Comic Art* (f) #3 1962?

My Day in Stir; or, Buried in the Tombs. *Village Voice* 9/29/60

My Life and Hard Times on a Casting Couch, by Terri Swinnerton as told to Jay Solo [pseud.] *Adam Bedside Reader* 2/67

Mystery Man Lucks and His Missing Bucks, as Ellis Hart. *Exposed* 8/56

The New American Woman [Anonymous]. *Esquire* 2/67 (*Very* edited; apa Kiss Me and You'll Live Forever)

Night Ride. *ItT* 11/8/57

Nightmare Nights at the Daisy. *LA* 9/66

No Fadeaway for This Old Soldier, a Three-War Vet. *ItT* 10/25/57

A Note on How This Story Came to Be Written. *F&SF* 10/76

The Novelist Comes to Television [with Theodore Sturgeon]. *Writer's Yearbook '67*

'One Kid's Kwestion' Gets Replies. *B&G* 10/8/52

The Opinion Bank: 14 Celebs Tell How Long They Expect to Live. *Moneysworth* 1/5/76

An Opinionated Thought. *Nyarlathotep* (f) 5/67

The Oscar. Cinema 12/65

Pro Guest of Honor: David Gerrold. *Oak-LA-Con 1/Westercon 28* [program book] (Oakland?: Westercon 28 Committee, 1976)

PX Writers Guild Shows Progress. *ItT* 1/31/58

Reaping the Whirlwind. *Fantasy Crossroads* (f) 8/75

Responses. *Khatru* (f) 2/75

Revealed at Last! What Killed the Dinosaurs! And You Don't Look So Terrific Yourself. *The 1978 National English Teachers' Symposium Notebook* (Santa Ana, CA: Professional Symposiums, 1978)

Rogue About Town: Bill of Fare, U.S.A.-Seattle, Washington [Anonymous]. *Rogue* 1/62

The Role of the Science Fiction Writer in the Visual Medium/O papel do escritor de ficcao cientifica no meio visual. *SF Symposium/FC Simposio,* ed. José Sanz (Rio de Janeiro: Istituto Nacional do Cinema, 1969)

Scherzo for Schizoids: Notes on a Collaboration. *Kt* 11/65

School for Apprentice Sorcerers. *St. Louiscon Program Book* (St. Louis: St. Louiscon, 27th World SF Convention, 1969)

Science Fiction and the Literary Scene [participant]. *Proceedings of the Day Program and* [Science Fiction Writers of America] *Nebula Awards Banquet: 1970,* ed. G. Benford (Philadelphia: Terminus, Owlswick & Ft. Mudge Electrick Street Railway Gazette, 1970?)

Science Fiction is for Teenagers, for Creeps, for Physicists, for Real. *New Times* 10/18/74

Science Fiction Write-In [contributor]. *Ingenue* 8/73

Secrets of a Sex Appeal School [Anonymous]. *MW* 5/56

7th Fandom Speaks. *Psy* (f) #15, 1954?

Seventh Fandom: The Dust was Thick. *Fanhistory* (f) 3/56

Shadow/Trickster: Some Afterthoughts on Delap's Nonfiction Fantasy by the Subject. *SFR* (f) 5/75

The Shocking Orgies of Italian Nobility, as Ellis Hart. *Exposed* 12/56

Showcase-Talents of Today [column]. *Rogue* 8/59 - 8/60

The Sick Chicks of Hollywood, as Ellis Hart. *Adam* 7 (9), 1963

Soldier-Scribe Chronicles Key 10th AD Role in War II. *ItT* 9/6/57

"Somehow, I Don't Think We're in Kansas, Toto." *Genesis* 6/74

Speaking Out: *Star Wars. Gallery* 3/78

Speculative Fiction: Out of the Ghetto. *Writer's Yearbook 1972*

Spero Meliora: Footnotes to an Adrenalin Flow [column]. *Introspection* (f) 9/64

The Staff of Life. *ItT* 11/7/58

The Starlost (Hollywood, CA: Dage, 1974/75?) 44 *1*. ("The word," "The bible" for the TV series)

A Statement of Ethical Position by the Worldcon Guest of Honor. *Locus* 12/77

A Statement of Posture; or, Harlan Ellison for the Greater Good. (Los Angeles: Al Lewis, 1964) 2 *1*.

Stealing Tomorrow. *Trumpet* (f) #11, 1974

Steve McQueen: Centerpunching. *Eye* 2/69

Sundial Christmas Gift Suggestions. *Sundial* 12/53

Talking Shop with Esquire [Anonymous]. *Sundial* 5/54

The Teenie Boppers: Where They're At! *Kt* 1/67

The Terminal Man. Mediascene (f) 5-6/74

The Terminal Man. Vertex 6/74

That Moon Plaque. *Men on the Moon,* ed. D.A. Wollheim (NY: Ace, 1969)

Them or Us: An Admittedly Opinionated Survey of the Past, Present and Future of Science Fiction in the Movies. *Show* 4/70

These are My Dreams. *Harlan Ellison: The Man-The Writer,* ed. H.

Devore (Detroit: Bloodstone Press for 1968 Detroit Triple Fan Fair, 1968)

Those Crazy Capers in the Social Register, as Ellis Hart. *Exposed* 9/56

Those Orientation Week Blues. *The New Nu News* [Newsletter of the Nu Chapter of Zeta Beta Tau] 10/31/53

Thoughts from Deep Space. *Psy* (f), 2/54; 4/54

Thoughts on Turning 18. *Crawdaddy* 6/75

3 Faces of Fear. *Cinema* 3/66

A Time for Daring. *Algol* (f) #12, 1967 (speech at Westercon 19, 1966)

Today, Young Hoods! Tomorrow-What? as Phil "Cheech" Beldone. *Lowdown* 10/55 (Ellison's 'gang name' and photo, but text is not his)

Toni: Affair with a Call Girl, as Bert Parker. *Kt* 9/67

Touché [Anonymous]. *Rogue* 4/60

True Yule Spirit Drops from Sky for Ky. Orphans. *ItT* 12/26/58

The Truth about Writing for Television: Shadow and Reality in Clown Town. *WD* 6/63; 7/63

Truth and the Writer. *Writer's Yearbook 1961*

Two Experimental Gadgets Help Training, Cut Costs. *ItT* 2/21/58

The Uncrowned King of Bourbon, as Robert Courtney. *Rogue* 3/60

Up to My Muffins. *Enclave* (f), 5-6/64

The Vampire Cult Still Lives [Anonymous]. *MW* 5/56

Vector: Two Attempts at Story. *Tomorrow and . . .* 1/69

Video Voyeurism. *Adam* 9/70

Voe, Doe, Dee, Oh, Doe (A Silverberg Medley), Recorded by the L.A. Syntopicon Syncopaters (Harlan Ellison & His Orchestra) Victor 22600. *Suncon* [Program Book] (Miami Beach: SunCon, 35th World SF Convention, 1977)

Voice from the Styx. *Stellar* 21, combined with *Gafia* #17, and *Dimensions* (f) 1958?

A Voice from the Styx [column]. *Psy* (f) 12/67; 1/68; 1/68

Voices 2: Harlan Ellison. *Colloquy* 5/71

A Warning from Another World. *The Wittenburg University Torch*, 10/4/73

What Do Women Really Mean When They Say NO! [Anonymous]. *MW* 4/56

What is the Sound of One Hippie Loving? as Matthew Quinton. *Cad* 2/68

What S-F Means to Me. *Vanations* (f) 11/52

When Dreams Become Nightmares: Some Cautionary Notes on the Clarion Experience. *Clarion III: An Anthology of Speculative Fiction and Criticism,* ed. Robin Scott Wilson (NY: NAL, 1973)

The Whimper of Whipped Dogs: 3 Film Variations. *Algol* Spring 1978

The Whore with a Heart of Iron Pyrites; or, Where Does a Writer Go to Find a Maggie? *Those Who Can: A Science Fiction Reader,* ed. Robin Scott Wilson (NY: NAL, 1973)

Why a Top Fantasy Writer Hates *Star Wars. LA* 8/77

Why Women Blow Men's Minds, as Jay Solo. *Kt* 3/68

With the Eyes of a Demon: Writing for Television Today. *WD* 7/76

Woman: Fine Art in Eight Parts. *FM & Fine Arts* 11/68

Wonder-Filled Christmas Opera 'Amahl and the Night Visitors' Has Quartet Sparkling Ballerinas as Well as Singers. *ItT* 11/28/58

The Wonderful World of Comic Books [participant]. *Kipple* (f) 1/10/61

The Words in Spock's Mouth. *Chatter Boxes* (f) 3-4/68

Writing [column]. *UnEarth* Summer 77; Fall 77

You Are What You Write. *Clarion II: An Anthology of Speculative Fiction and Criticism,* ed. Robin Scott Wilson (NY: NAL, 1972)

"You Could Split Behind a Lug That Heavy." *Eye* 10/68

You Don't Know Me, I Don't Know You. *F&SF* 7/77

Your Card Reads Black Sheep, as Robert Courtney. *Rogue* 12/59

INTRODUCTIONS & AFTERWORDS

Harlan has contributed introductions and afterwords not only to his own books and stories but also to those of others. He has contributed an introduction and/or afterword to nearly all of his own books, namely: *Alone Against Tomorrow* (1971), *Approaching Oblivion* (1974), *The Beast That Shouted Love at the Heart of the World* (1969), *The Deadly Streets* (1958), *Deathbird Stories* (1976), *Ellison Wonderland* (1962), *From the Land of Fear* (1967), *Gentleman Junkie* (1961), *I Have No Mouth and I Must Scream* (1967), *The Juvies* (1961), *Love Ain't Nothing But Sex Misspelled* (1968), *No Doors, No Windows* (1975), *Over the Edge* (1970), *Paingod* (1965), *Partners in Wonder* (1971), *Phoenix Without Ashes* [with Edward Bryant] (1975), *Spider Kiss* [originally: *Rockabilly*] (1961), *A Touch of Infinity* (1960), and *Web of the City* [originally: *Rumble*] (1958). The only three of his books to which he did not contribute an introduction and/or an afterword are *Doomsman* (1967), *De Helden Van De Highway* (1973), and *The Man With Nine Lives* (1960). For details on these books of fiction, please see my checklist in *F&SF,* July 1977.

He has written introductions and/or afterwords to his own stories, either the original or reprint publication, namely for:

Catman. *Final Stage: The Ultimate Science Fiction Anthology,* ed. E.L. Ferman & B.N. Malzberg (NY: Charterhouse, 1974)
The City on the Edge of Forever [script]. *Six Science Fiction Plays,* ed. R. Elwood (NY: Washington Square Press, 1976)
Demon With a Glass Hand [excerpts]. *Harlan Ellison: The Man-The Writer,* ed. H. Devore (Detroit: Bloodstone Press for the 1968 Detroit Triple Fan Fair, 1968)
Glowworm. *UnEarth* Winter 77
I Have No Mouth, and I Must Scream. *A Pocketful of Stars,* ed. D. Knight (NY: Doubleday, 1971)
The New York Review of Bird. *Weird Heroes: Volume 2,* ed. B. Preiss (NY: Pyramid, 1975)
O Ye of Little Faith. *SF: Author's Choice 3,* ed. H. Harrison (NY: Putnam, 1971)
Phoenix Without Ashes [script]. *Faster Than Light,* ed. J. Dann & G. Zebrowski (NY: Harper & Row, 1976)
Silent in Gehenna. *The Future Now: Saving Tomorrow,* ed. R. Hoskins (Greenwich, CT: Fawcett, 1977)
Soldier [script]. *A Mixed Bag* (2nd ed), ed. A. Casty (Englewood Cliffs, NJ: Prentice-Hall, 1975)

He has also contributed introductions and/or afterwords to books which he edited, namely to a collection:
Kersh, The Demon Prince. *Nightshade & Damnations,* by Gerald Kersh (NY: Fawcett, 1968)
to his two anthologies:
Dangerous Visions: 33 Original Stories (Garden City, NY: Doubleday, 1967)
Again, Dangerous Visions: 46 Original Stories (Garden City, NY: Doubleday, 1972)
and to the volumes of the *Harlan Ellison Discovery Series:*
#1: Gale Warning. *Stormtrack,* by James Sutherland (NY: Pyramid, 1974)
#2: The $\Phi\Psi\Omega$ [phi psy omega] of A B C.*Autumn Angels,* by Arthur Byron Cover (NY: Pyramid, 1975)
#3: Nice Guys Finish Somewhere in the Middle. *The Light at the End of the Universe,* by Terry Carr (NY: Pyramid, 1976)
#4: A Fineness of 0.995. *Involution Ocean,* by Bruce Sterling (NY: Jove/HBJ, 1977)

Finally, he has contributed introductions and afterwords to the works of others, namely to:

Ravished, by Richard E. Geis (No. Hollywood, CA: Essex House, 1968)

Daily Survivor, by Tony Isabella, Carla Joseph, Gerry Conway, and Steve Skeates. *Crazy* 10/73

Nine by Laumer, by Keith Laumer (NY: Doubleday, 1967)

The Tour: Hell's Heated Vacancies, by Michael Perkins (No. Hollywood, CA: Essex House, 1969)

Lone Star Universe: The First Anthology of Texas Science Fiction Authors, ed. G.W. Proctor & S. Utley (Austin: Heidelberg, 1976)

Season of the Witch, by Hank Stine (No. Hollywood, CA: Essex House, 1968)

Harlan Ellison: A Bibliographical Checklist, by L.K. Swigart (Dallas: Williams, 1973)

Anthology of Slow Death, ed. B.R. Turner (np: Wingbow Press, 1975)

REVIEWS

Harlan has contributed reviews of books (b), films (f), magazines & comics (m), plays & concerts (p), and records (r) to a number of magazines and newspapers.

B&G 9/26/51 (f)

Cad 12/65; 3/66; 6/66; 9/66; 1/67; 3/67; 5/67; 7/67 (r)

Cinema 7-8/65; 12/65; 3/66; 7/66; Winter 67; Fall 68 (f)

Delap's F & SF Review (f) 8/75; 9/76; 4/77; 2/78 (b, r)

The Hollywood Reporter 9/26/77 (b)

ItT 11/29/57; 12/6/57; 12/13/57; 12/20/57; 12/24/57; 1/3/58; 1/10/58; 1/24/58; 2/7/58; 2/28/58; 10/31/58; 12/19/58 (b, p)

JG: Jazz Guide 8/60 (r)

LAFP 3/26/65; 5/16-22/69; 6/5-11/70; 9/25/70; 3/19-25/71; 4/16-22/71 (b, f, p)

LAT 12/21/71; 7/3/72 (b)

LAT. Book Review 4/19/70; 10/25/70; 4/25/71; 11/28/71; 11/10/74; 5/25/75; 11/23/75; 7/11/76; 9/18/77 (b)

LAT. Books 2/15/70 (b)

LAT. Calendar 4/20/69; 1/4/70; 6/28/70; 8/2/70; 8/16/70; 3/14/71; 4/18/71; 5/9/71; 7/2/72; 7/9/72; 12/30/73; 12/15/74; 2/23/75 (b)

F&SF 6/71; 1/74; 5/74 (b)

Newfangles (f) 10/68 (m)

The Pendulum (f) 5-6/52; 9/52 (m)

Rogue 11/59; 12/60; 1/61; 4/61; 9/61; 1/62 (r, p)

The Staff [Los Angeles] 9/10/71; 9/17/71; 10/1-7/71; 3/31-4/6/72; 1/19-26/73; 2/16-22/73; 3/2-8/73; 3/23-29/73 (b, f, p)
Swank 7/61; 9/61; 11/61 (r)
33 Guide: Monthly Reviews & Ratings of 100 New Pop, Jazz, and Folk Record Albums 6/61; 7/61 (r)
Topper 5/63; 6/63; 7/63; 8/63 (r)
Trumpet (f) #9, 1969 (f)
WGAW 12/71; 1/72; 3/72; 11/72; 5/73; 2/74; 4/74 (b)
Xero (f) 9/60 (f)

LETTERS

Harlan has had letters published in numerous professional and fan magazines.

The Alien Critic (f) 5/73; 11/73; 2/74; 5/74
Analog 1/74
Aniara (f) 7/9/76
¡Ay, Chingar! (f) 5/75
Bane (f) #3, 1961?
The Best is Yet to Come! Masterminded by Jackie Franke & Bill Bowers (f) 1976
Cleveland News 4/20/49
Conan the Barbarian 12/70
Crawdaddy 3/77
Crazy 12/74
Crossroads (f) 7/69; 9/69
Cthulhu Calls 1/74
Detective Comics 10/68
Fantastic 10/57; 7/74; 11/74
The Forever People 6-7/71
Inside (f) 6/63
Inside-Riverside Quarterly (f) Summer 64
Introspection (f) 8/62; 8/63; 9/64
Janus (f) 3/76
The Jinnia Clan Journal (f) 4-5/75
Khatru (f) 11/75
Knight, Damon. *Best Stories from Orbit, Volumes 1-10* (NY: Berkley/Putnam, 1975)
LAFP 12/15-25/72
Mathom (f) 10/69
F&SF 4/75
New Venture (f) #2, 1975

Nite Cry (f) 8/54; 1/55; #10, 1955
No (f) 3/73
Other Worlds SF 1/52
Oui 9/75; 4/77
Outworlds (f) 6/73
Psy (f) #12, 1954; 12/67; 5/68
Quantum (f) 2 (3), 1977
Rogue 12/60; 5/61
Savage Sword of Conan 12/74
Science Fiction Adventures 12/57
SFR 8/55; 9/55; 11/68; 4/69; 2/76; 5/76; 8 [sic, 11]/76; 5/77; 11/77;
     5/78
SFWA Forum 11/71; 1/73; 4/19/73; 12/75
Scientifriction (f) 9/75
Speculation (f) 2/69
Starlog 12/77
Swamp Thing 9-10/73
TV Guide 9/25/71
The Third Degree [Mystery Writers of America] 12/74
2-5YM (f) 9/75
Washington S.F. Association Journal (f) 6-7/71
WD 9/63; 12/76
WGAW 1/72; 4/72; 4/76

INTERVIEWS

Harlan has been interviewed innumerable times. The listing below is arranged by the interviewer and gives the place of first publication.

[Anonymous]. *Foundation* 4-7/75
[Anonymous]. *If* 3/69
[Anonymous]. *Mystery Monthly* 1/76
Bly, Robert, Rick Link, & Laura Sechrist. *Logos* [U. of Rochester]
     4/21/77
Bunch, Chris. *Los Angeles Image* 9/19-10/2/69
Burkhardt, Chris. *The Western Herald Twang* [Western Michigan U.,
     Kalamazoo] 11/15/74]
Cover, Arthur Byron. *Vertex* 4/74
Cowan, James. *S-S-F* [U. of Wisconsin, Milwaukee] Spring 1974
Duvic, Patrice. *Nueva Dimension* 2/72
Efron, Edith. *TV Guide* 8/3/74
Evans, Sharon. *Horizons du Fantastique* #37, 1975
Fowler, Chris. *Vector* (f) 7/76

Garst, Ron. *San Francisco Ball* #47, 1972?

Hartwell, David G. *Crawdaddy* 5/73

Lampton, Chris. *Thrust* (f) Spring 76

McGrath, Paul. *The* [Toronto] *Globe and Mail.* Fanfare 12/7/77

Moreland, James. *Youngblood* (f) 11/76

McKay, Nancy. *The Dallas Sun* 3/77

Silver, Diane. *State News* [Michigan State U., E. Lansing] 7/19/74

Snyder, Tom. *Transcript of the Tomorrow Show, March 15, 1976, Featuring Guest Harlan Ellison* (Portland, OR: Foray Press, 1976) 20 p.

Swires, Steve. *Take One* 10/76

Turner, Alice K. *Publishers Weekly* 2/10/75

Williams, Joe Bob. *DJ: DaSFS* [Dallas Science Fiction Society] *Journal* (f) 6/69

Wyman, Rich, and Bob Harloran. *Starwind* (f) Autumn 77

Zimmerman, Howard. *Starlog* 9/77

For complete catalog of publications, write:
ALGOL Press
P.O. Box 4175
New York, NY 10017